Sherlock Holmes:
The Synchrony Stratagem

Sinister House Book 3

by

James Patrick Heatherly

Hardcover ISBN 978-1-80424-435-7
Paperback ISBN 978-1-80424-436-4
ePub ISBN 978-1-80424-437-1
PDF ISBN 978-1-80424-438-8

Published by MX Publishing
335 Princess Park Manor, Royal Drive,
London, N11 3GX
www.mxpublishing.co.uk

Cover design by Brian Belanger

For My Family

Annamae, I found the muse.

Acknowledgements

Heartfelt thanks to Judith Laughlin, who helped tremendously, keeping me on task and being the first to read and critique this work. Her careful and often unvarnished observations helped make this a better work. Further, I am deeply indebted to Richard Ryan whose fastidious editing and unwavering defense of the Holmes legacy helped me stay true to the Doyle Canon. Without his meticulous oversight, this book may never have seen the light of day. Deepest appreciation to Steve Emecz of MX Publishing for his indefatigable patience and support of a first-time novelist. And, thanks to Tim Hubbard of the Arthur Conan Doyle Estate, whose faith in this work will never be forgotten.

While I have borrowed a smidge from Charles Dickens, Wilkie Collins, and Edgar Allan Poe, this work could never have been written had it not been for the enduring brilliance of Sir Arthur Conan Doyle. As a boy of eleven, I first discovered the world of Sherlock Holmes, and I have been entertained and fascinated by the stories of the famed detective my entire life. Adding to the body of work that is the world of Sherlock Holmes has been a dream of mine since I picked up my first Holmes story. It has truly been a labor of love. I only hope I have honored the original Doyle Canon with this addition.

PROLOGUE

Sherlock Holmes had deciphered the clues that led him and his colleagues to get a step or two closer to uncovering the most sinister organization he has ever faced. However, once the threats against Queen Victoria's son, the Prince of Wales, and her grandson, Kaiser Wilhelm II of the German Empire had been quashed, Holmes realized there were yet new and ever more devastating threats to be tackled. Assassination attempts against Queen Victoria and President Carnot of France were in the works. If successful, these events could very well result in a domino effect, wreaking havoc on the stability of all of Europe.

Again, racing against time, and this time facing challenges in England and France, Holmes realized the task was formidable. He could not be in two places at the same time. Worse still, both assassination attempts were to take place on the same day and time.

Holmes turned to his brother, Mycroft, to assist him in assembling a team of associates, in hopes they could be relied on to stop the impending events. To address the potential assassination attempt in Paris, Mycroft introduced Holmes to a young man familiar with the Surete by the name of Algernon Quartermaine. Partnered with his old friend, Ormond Sacker, the two men would have to devise a plan to identify and neutralize the assassins before they could accomplish their nefarious deeds. To nullify the impending assassination attempt on the life of Queen Victoria, Holmes assembled another cadre of associates. This included covert agents in the employ of Mycroft, Nathaniel Hobbs and Jonah Burke, and, of course, his trusted colleague, John Watson.

Notwithstanding the overwhelming odds stacked against them, the intrepid teams in England and in France succeeded in learning the identities of the assassins, placed themselves in harm's way, and stopped the murderers from accomplishing their deadly plans.

But, despite the efforts of Holmes and his compatriots, the criminal enterprise had yet another surprise up its sleeve. Holmes once again faces a new provocation. But, if successful in thwarting this new challenge, he may finally uncover the genius behind the mayhem and learn the identity of the master of this Sinister House.

CHAPTER ONE

In the Aftermath

There was a palpable sense of tension within the offices of the Prefecture of Police. Outside, reporters from *Le Temps, Le Petit Journal, Le Matin*, and *Le Petit Parisien* had all gathered, and were rather raucously demanding entrance to speak to the prefect. Inside, Henri Loze had been called to the office of Chief Goron to discuss how and what to say to the reporters clamoring for information for their evening editions regarding the incident at the Eiffel dedication, and the explosions at the Louvre and the Banque de France.

"I need to know what you are planning to tell the reporters, Henri."

"Chief Inspector, I think it best we tell them as little as possible. So, unless you order me to do otherwise, that is my plan."

Chief Inspector Goron paused for a moment, contemplating what Loze had just said. "What exactly are you intending to say, then, Henri?"

"Exactly, sir? Well, of that I am yet unsure. But, I can assure you of that which I am not going to tell them. I am not going to tell them that our men thwarted assassination attempts on the lives of President Carnot and Prime Minister Floquet. Nor am I going to tell them that the Banque de France was robbed of a king's ransom this afternoon."

"Then how are you going to explain what has transpired this afternoon, Henri?"

"With all due respect, sir, I am going to bend the truth. I think it is imperative if we are going to have any chance and hope of catching the criminals who perpetrated these crimes."

Goron stared at Henri Loze for a minute. Then, he plopped into his chair and waved his hand. "Do what you think is best, Henri. I leave this in your capable hands."

"Thank you, sir. One last thing before I go. Am I free to select whomever I choose to work this new investigation?"

"I suppose you already have men in mind?"

"I do indeed, sir."

"Do as you see fit, Henri. Just get the job done. Just keep me apprised of your progress. There is much at stake here, not the least of which is our continued employment."

"Yes, sir. I will do my best, sir." Henri Loze closed the door and headed back to his own office. His mind raced with thoughts of what to say to the reporters. He walked to the front desk and pulled the young gendarme aside. "Aubin, I need you to go out to the reporters and tell them that I will have an announcement for them in one hour. They are welcome to wait outside, or return in an hour. Their choice. But, under no circumstances are you to allow any of them inside this office. Am I clear."

"Yes, sir. I will do as you order immediately." The young gendarme went out to the group of reporters waiting on the front steps and explained the situation. There was a boisterous response, with a number of the reporters demanding to speak directly with Prefect Loze. The young gendarme apologized and once more explained the situation. Then he turned, went back into the office, and locked the front doors.

An hour passed, and finally Henri Loze went out to face the querulous group of reporters. He raised his hands to quieten the group. "Gentlemen, thank you for waiting so patiently. I have information for you regarding this afternoon's events. Unfortunately, after I provide my remarks, I will not be answering any questions. As more information comes to my attention, I will, of course, be willing to speak with all of you again. But, for now, this is what I can tell you. With regard to the incident at the Eiffel dedication this afternoon, one individual was subdued by officers of the Surete. Based on identification of the man after he was taken away, it was determined that he was one of two men who had escaped from the Sainte-Anne asylum a few days previously. It appears that, while in custody in hospital, he had been ranting about the upcoming Exposition and had become very agitated. While President Carnot was making his remarks, this man appeared and began to move forward through the crowd. When he drew a weapon, he was subdued before he could do any harm to anyone. One of our officers was injured while trying to subdue the man, but he is alive and well. Thankfully, no one else was injured."

Some of the reporters raised their hands to ask questions, and one or two shouted for more information. Henri Loze raised his hands again. "Gentlemen, please. No questions. That is all I can tell you at present about that incident."

"What about the explosion at the Louvre?" one reporter called out.

"Ah, yes. Well, let us deal with that next. As I said, two men escaped from Sainte-Anne. The man who caused a disturbance at the Louvre this afternoon appears to be the second man. At present, it is our speculation that he saw the large gathering of people and, somehow, made his way inside. At some point after the prime minister had concluded his dedication of the Rembrandt exhibit, the man took a small explosive device from his coat pocket, shouted something unintelligible, and then committed suicide by blowing himself up. Once again, thankfully, no one else was injured. There was some minor damage to the floor and walls in the hall, but none of the masterpieces were harmed."

"What can you tell us about the explosion at Banque de France, Monsieur Loze?" asked a reporter from *Le Petit Parisien.*

Loze paused for a moment, sizing up the target of his next remarks. "First let me say, what I am about to tell you will not satisfy your readers, Monsieur Mirbeau. I am afraid it is not quite sensational enough for your paper. However, this is the information I have for you to publish. This afternoon, at the Banque de France, there was a small fire. It was caused by the malfunction of two gas lamps. Based on information I have received from one of our gendarmes, who spoke with the captain of the fire brigade who responded to the fire, there was a rupture of the gas lines to two of the lamps, which caused a small blast and ensuing fire. The fire was quickly contained and there were no reported injuries. That is all I can tell you about that incident at present."

One of the reporters called out, "So there was no attempted bank robbery?"

Loze ignored the query and held up his hands one more. "Gentlemen. Gentlemen. I have given you all the information I am going to give you about these three incidents. When more information becomes available, you will be notified by someone in my office. Thank you for your kind attention. Adieu." As the reporters shouted their questions, Loze turned and went back inside.

*   *   *   *   *

Quartermaine and Rene Perrault sat on a bench in the open courtyard of Necker Hospital, patiently waiting, while Jacques Duquesne paced back-and-forth on the flagstone walk, looking up every so often to see if one of the Sisters of Mercy was coming to offer any information on their colleagues being tended to inside. "Jacques, please sit down," Rene said, pleadingly. "You are making me nervous."

"Why is it taking so long? We have been here two hours, and no one has told us anything about their conditions."

"This is a busy place, Jacques," Quartermaine replied. "I am sure someone will come out to tell us something when there is something to tell."

"I think one of us should go inside and see what is taking so long."

"Sacker!" exclaimed Quartermaine and Rene simultaneously, jumping to their feet.

Sacker came up behind Jacques and patted him on the back. Jacques turned around and, happy to see his colleague, he hugged him, nearly lifting him off the ground.

"Ooof…easy, Jacques, easy. I don't want to have to go back and have them stitch me up again."

"So, you are all right?" Quartermaine asked, honestly concerned for his colleague's well-being.

Sacker walked over to the bench and sat down. "They put in a few stitches. So long as no one picks me up and squeezes the life out of me, I will be fine." He reached into his pocket and took out a clean handkerchief, which had been folded very carefully. "You need to see this." He opened the handkerchief and in it was a small bit of bloody cloth and a tiny shard of indeterminate matter.

"What is it?" Rene asked.

"The doctor took that out of my wound. It seems when that little vixen stabbed me, a piece of my shirt went into the wound, along with this other sliver of my rib, nicked off by that nasty little blade she stuck me with. The doctor said if he hadn't pulled them out, gangrene could have set into the wound. He said he learned that from a friend of his, a gentleman by the name of Pasteur. I will tell you, though, him digging around in my side hurt much worse than the stitches."

"But you are all right, and that is all that matters," Quartermaine said.

"Did you get a chance to ask about Remy or Louis?" Jacques asked, anxiously.

"As I headed down the hallway, I passed a room where Remy was having his head bandaged. He was sitting up and, best I could tell, he was alert. What happened to him?"

"He was shot in the head by Cingle," Quartermaine replied.

"Then he should be just fine," Rene said, jokingly. "Nothing could hurt that *tête de citrouille.*"

They all laughed, and Sacker clutched his side. "Don't make me laugh. It hurts too much."

11

"What is so funny?" Remy asked, as he approached, head tightly wrapped with a bandage. The men all turned to see their friend and colleague approaching. There was another burst of laughter.

"We are just happy to see you, Remy," Rene said, stifling his amusement.

"It is good to see you on your feet, Remy. Do you know if they have taken care of Louis?"

"I do not know, Jacques, I am sorry to say. Hasn't one of the Sisters of Mercy come out to tell you anything?"

"No one has told us anything, and we have been here two hours."

"Jacques, you said his wound went clean through his shoulder. He is a strong man. He should be fine," Quartermaine responded. "It would just take time to close that wound. But, if it will ease your mind, I will go in and ask as to his current situation."

"I would be most grateful."

Sacker got up and walked over to Quartermaine. "While you're in there, if you wouldn't mind, see if you can find out what happened to our mad bomber."

"I will do that," Quartermaine replied, turning and heading into the hospital.

A quarter hour passed, and Quartermaine finally came out of the hospital with Louis at his side. Louis's left arm was in a sling, but he seemed well in all other respects. The men all surrounded their colleague, and Louis noted it was the first time since breakfast they had all been together. "Is there any chance we could go back and get some more of those croissants? I am famished."

Jacques looked at his friend incredulously, then smiled. "You have been shot, helped to stop an assassination attempt on the president, and all you can think of is your stomach. That is the Louis I know."

Sacker walked over to Quartermaine and whispered, "Any word on Michel Dubois?"

"One word. Deceased."

"Then we have taken care of all of the villains, save one."

"Sleeves?"

"Yes, Sleeves. Do you think he is foolish enough to have stayed in Paris?"

"There is one way to find out. We could pay him a visit at his hotel. If he has checked out, we know he is running again. If he is there, I will leave it to you how we deal with him."

Sacker turned to his colleagues. "Gentlemen, Algernon and I have some unfinished business to attend to. Is there somewhere we can meet up later this evening to celebrate our success?"

"Wherever you wish, monsieur," Jacques replied. "You select the time and place, and we will be there."

"Well, I am no connoisseur, by any stretch of the imagination. But a docent at the Louvre told me of a place, which I thoroughly enjoyed. If you have no objections, we could meet at Le Procope at eight this evening."

"Le Procope?" exclaimed Jacques. "No connoisseur indeed. That is one of the finest restaurants in all of Paris. We will be most happy to join you there. On one condition," Jacques said, winking at his colleagues.

Sacker looked at Quartermaine, "Am I in for it?"

"You are," replied his friend, smiling. "They expect you to pay the bill."

"Done. Since Algernon and I have pressing business elsewhere, and we are unsure of how long it may take, please get a table for six at eight o'clock. We will do our best to be on time, but do not wait on us."

"Do you need any help with your pressing business?"

"Thank you, Jacques, but no. This matter is personal for me. Algernon is accompanying me to finish the job in the event I fail. We will see you at eight, or thereabouts." With that Sacker and Algernon left their colleagues and headed for the street where they could flag a cabriolet.

"Are you sure you are up for this?"

"Are you sure your pistol is loaded? If it is, we are both ready." A cab pulled up and the two men climbed in. Sacker called up to the driver, "228 Rue De Rivoli."

When the cab came to a stop in front of Hotel Le Meurice, Sacker and Quartermaine climbed out. Sacker paid the driver, as Quartermaine strode over to the doorman and whispered something to him, pushing a five franc coin into his palm. As Sacker approached, Quartermaine joined him and the doorman opened the door. The two men crossed the lobby to the front desk and an impeccably dressed young man greeted them. "Bonsoir, messieurs. Comment puis-je vous aider?"

"Parlez-vous couramment anglaise?" Quartermaine asked.

The desk manager smiled. "Oui, monsieur. Je parle aussi italien, allemande et neerlandais."

"English will be quite enough for us, thank you."

"How may I be of service?"

Quartermaine put his hand on Sacker's shoulder, "My friend here has been looking all over Paris for a former compatriot of his from the British Army. Isn't that so, William?"

"That is so. My name is William Paton, former sergeant major of the Royal Horse Artillery of the Bengal Army, under the command of Major George Blackwood. The last time I saw my friend was before the taking of the fortress at Kandahar. One of our fellow gunners has recently passed and he gave me a token to give to our mate. I am desperate to find him. We have tried nearly every hotel in Paris. This is our last hope. Could you please see if you have anyone by the name of George Harrington Sleeves staying here?"

"Monsieur Sleeves, but of course. Quite a gentleman. He has been here for quite some time now. And you are most fortunate to have come this evening, messieurs. Sadly, Monsieur Sleeves has informed us he will be leaving us in the morning. He is returning to his country estate in England."

"His country estate, you say? Well, my old compatriot Sleeves has done much better than this poor old gunnery sergeant, I must say. I am happy for him."

Quartermaine leaned over the desk and quietly asked, "Is there any chance my friend and I could go up to his room and surprise him? It would mean the world to my friend there."

"I can see no harm in that. I am sure Monsieur Sleeves will be happy to see his old friend. I will have our bellman take you to Monsieur Sleeves' suite."

"That will not be necessary. If you will just tell us his suite number, we will find our way. We want it to be a big surprise."

"Are you sure, monsieur? It would be no trouble for the bellman to take you up." .

"Quite sure, monsieur," Quartermaine replied, emphatically.

As the two men rode the hydraulic lift to the sixth floor, Quartermaine turned to Sacker, "Ormond, you realize Sleeves will likely come to the door with a pistol?"

"I am fully aware of that possibility. That is why I asked you to make sure your revolver is loaded. When we get to his door, I will need you to stand out of sight. I want him to think I came alone."

"And if he shoots you?"

"Then you shoot him. But let us hope it does not come to that. Holmes wants him brought back to London unharmed for questioning. It will be hard to question him if he is deceased."

"I would assume so. You know, Ormond, you have a very perverse sense of humour."

"So I have been told," Sacker replied, pulling back the gate and stepping out of the lift. He walked with Quartermaine to the middle of the hallway. When they came to Sleeves' suite, Quartermaine drew his revolver and pressed his back to the wall, out of view from the doorway. Sacker knocked on the door.

Sleeves opened the door wide and took a step back. His pistol was pointed at whoever was standing in the doorway. "You. How did you find me?"

"I am cleverer than you give me credit for, Sleeves. All of the assassins have been dispatched. I have come for my payment."

Sleeves lowered his pistol and walked over and closed the door. He paused for a moment, trying to think of what to say. "I don't have much cash with me in the room. Certainly not enough to pay you. I can meet you at Banque de France in the morning, if you can wait until then."

"Would that be before or after you depart for your country estate in England?"

Sleeves started to raise his pistol again, but Sacker moved swiftly toward him, punching him square in the face. Sleeves fell back, clipping the back of his head on an oaken side table on the way down. He was unconscious when he hit the floor. Sacker walked to the door and opened it. Quartermaine was standing in the hallway, his pistol leveled chest high. "You can put that away. Sleeves isn't going to give us any trouble," Sacker said, pointing at the insensible Sleeves lying on the floor behind him. "You could help me truss him up, though. I think it will be much easier while he is still napping."

When Sleeves finally awakened, he found himself gagged, his hands tied behind his back. Sacker and Quartermaine were seated in armchairs in front of him. "Nod if you can understand me," Sacker said. Sleeves nodded he understood. Sacker leaned forward and stared directly at Sleeves. "Listen, carefully. This is what is going to happen. We are going to walk out of your room, just three old Bengal Army chums going out for a drink. You will still have your hands tied, but I am going to take off your gag. As we walk out of the hotel, you are not to say a word. My colleague is going to be holding a pistol against your ribs. If you make a sound, he is going to put a bullet in you. Nod if you understand." Sleeves nodded his understanding. Sacker rose from his chair and motioned for Quartermaine to follow. The two men walked across the room, out of earshot of Sleeves. "I'm not sure I thought this plan all the way through, Algie. Any suggestions what we do with him once we get him outside?"

"Actually, I do. As we entered the hotel, I paid the doorman five francs to flag down a carriage. I told him there would be another five francs in it for him if the carriage were waiting for us when we came out. Once we get Sleeves out the front door, I will wager there will be a carriage waiting for us."

"Good man!" Sacker walked back to where Sleeves was seated on the floor. "Shall we, then?"

Quartermaine walked over and helped Sacker hoist Sleeves to his feet. "Hang on a moment," he said, walking to the closet and retrieving Sleeves overcoat. He placed it over Sleeves' shoulders. "No point in letting everyone know what we are up to now, is there?" The three men exited the suite. Sacker closed the door, and they walked casually to the lift. They rode the lift to the lobby and started across to the front doors. The desk manager called out from behind the front desk, "Monsieur Sleeves, have a wonderful evening with your friends." Sleeves turned his head and was about to reply when he felt the barrel of Quartermaine's revolver press into his ribcage. They exited the hotel and, as planned, there was a carriage waiting. The doorman ran ahead of the three men and opened the carriage door. Quartermaine reached into his pocket and took out a ten franc gold coin and gave it to the doorman. "Merci beaucoup, mon ami," he said, climbing into the carriage. Then he knocked on the roof of the cab and call up to the driver, "One Rue de Lutece, Place Louis Lepine, s'il vous plait." The carriage pulled away, and Quartermaine sat back in his seat across from Sleeves. "You may speak now, if you have anything to say."

"You both think you are so clever. You have no idea who I work for, or to what lengths they will go to assure they remain anonymous."

"Who you work for is precisely what we intend to learn from you," Sacker retorted. "And we know just the man to get information out of you."

"If you are referring to your revered Mister Sherlock Holmes, I am not afraid of him, or what he might do to me. It is nothing compared to what will happen to me if I snitch."

"Oh, you must be referring to what Colonel Moran will do to you? So, you are afraid you will end up like your lackey Hoder in Berlin? Not to worry. When we get you back to London, you are going to be put in a hole so dark and deep, it will be hard for the Good Lord to find you, never mind Colonel Moran."

"You fools," Sleeves chortled. "I will never make it back to London. And it is likely neither will either of you. Once it is learned I am in custody, I am a dead man. And if, by some quirk of fate, you get me on a boat to cross the channel, you will doom everyone aboard. The organization I work for takes their anonymity quite seriously. They will stop at nothing to preserve that. The smartest thing you could do right now is stop this carriage and let me go free."

"I think not," Sacker replied, taking a handkerchief from his pocket and jamming it into Sleeves' mouth. "And I think I have heard enough from you for now. Just sit there and be quiet."

When the carriage pulled up in front of 1 Rue de Lutece, Place Louis Lepine, Sacker climbed out of the carriage first, paid the driver, and then helped Sleeves climb down from the carriage. Quartermaine followed behind. They walked Sleeves into the police prefecture, and Quartermaine asked the desk sergeant if Prefect Loze was still in the building. The sergeant replied that Prefect Loze was still working in his office, noting the fact that two assassination attempts had been thwarted earlier in the day and there had been an explosion at Banque de France.

Quartermaine replied that he was aware of those events, but asked if the sergeant could go nonetheless and ask Prefect Loze if he had a few moments to speak with him. "It is of the utmost importance, sergeant. If you could tell Prefect Loze we have someone here who has intimate knowledge of the assassinations and we need a word."

The sergeant rose and went down the hall to the prefect's office. In a matter of minutes, the prefect came down the hall. "Algernon, if I had known it was you, I would have had the sergeant bring you back to my office. Come, come. Let us discuss this matter in private." He led the three men back to his office. Quartermaine took Sleeves by the arm and placed him in a chair in the corner. "Henri, this is my colleague, Ormond Sacker. He and I have been working with the men you assigned to me to thwart the assassinations."

"Ah, yes. Fine job you all did. How are Louis and Remy?"

"They are recovering from their wounds, Henri. But, more to the point, this man was responsible for recruiting the assassins," Quartermaine said, pointing at Sleeves. "And this is not the first time he has been involved in such affairs. My colleague has specific knowledge of this man's involvement in the attempt to assassinate Kaiser Wilhelm in Berlin, and we have suspicions that he was involved in planning an assassination attempt on Queen Victoria in England. By his own admission, his organization will stop at nothing to silence him. Can I trust him to your care until Ormond and I can arrange passage to England?"

"Why would you want to take him to England? He should stand trial here in Paris and, when convicted, he should meet his fate on the guillotine."

"Henri, please, I beg of you, think bigger. This man can provide information regarding a criminal organization that spans the Continent. We know virtually nothing about them. We only see the results of their actions after the fact, when it is too late to do anything about it. We must find out who these men are and do whatever we can to stop them. I want to bring this man to Sherlock Holmes, so he can interrogate him. Holmes has a theory about this organization, and I think this man can give him a missing piece to the puzzle. If you will help me, I promise I will bring this man back to stand trial when Mister Holmes is through with him. You have my word."

Henri Loze thought for a moment. "It is against my better judgment, Algernon. But you are an honorable man and I trust your word. I will hold him here overnight while you arrange passage."

"Thank you, Henri. One more thing. Can you incarcerate him without listing him in your register? I fear even listing him under an alias may draw undue attention. I am sure you have an empty cell somewhere that he could occupy for one night unnoticed."

"There are the old barracks for the Garde Républicaine; they are to be demolished soon. There are detention cells no longer in use. We could hide him there for the night. But to be sure no one knows he is there, you will have to take him there yourselves. Wait here, I will get the keys to the barracks."

By half seven, Sleeves was securely locked in a detention cell in the old barracks and Quartermaine and Sacker were on their way to Le Procope to join their colleagues for a sumptuous dinner. Sacker looked at his friend. "You know this is going to be no easy task getting Sleeves back to London. We have to get to Calais to take a boat to Dover, then we will have to figure some way to get from Dover to London without losing our prisoner."

"Ormond, can you rest your mind for a few hours at least. We may never see our colleagues again after tonight. So, let us enjoy their company and worry about what lies ahead after we say goodnight to our friends."

"As you wish." Sacker slumped back in his seat, falling deep into thought.

When Sacker and Quartermaine arrived at Le Procope, their colleagues had already been given a table near the back of the room. The conversation was jovial and boisterous, and there were two bottles of wine on the table, one lying on its side empty, the second with only half the burgundy remaining.

As they approached, the four men at the table cheered their colleagues and bade them sit and have something to drink. Jacques rose to his feet and raised a glass to propose a toast. "In the words of the great Frenchman, Alexandre Dumas, 'Great criminals bear about them a kind of predestination which makes them surmount all obstacles, which makes them escape all dangers, until the moment which a wearied Providence has marked as the rock for their impious fortunes.' To Providence."

"To Providence!" came the reply in unison.

In a quivering voice, Jacques added, "And to my brothers-in-arms at this table."

"To brothers-in-arms!" they all responded.

Louis looked at Jacques, who remained standing unsteadily. "Please sit, my friend, before you fall."

"I am steady as a rock," Jacques replied, plopping back into his chair.

"Jacques, I think it's time for a little food to go with that burgundy," Sacker quipped.

Jacques burped. "Pardon moi, mon ami. I think you are right." He attempted to snap his fingers twice, unsuccessfully, then just shouted, "Garcon, viens ici tout de suite, sit u veux."

The waiter came over to the table and each man made his dinner selection. As the waiter was about to leave, Quartermaine caught him by the arm. "No more wine until you bring our meals, please. And if you could bring bread and a pitcher of water to the table, we would all be most appreciative." The waiter nodded and departed for the kitchen.

By the time dinner was concluded, there were two more empty bottles of burgundy on the table, and Jacques was caressing a fifth nearly empty bottle in his arms like a baby. Sacker rose to pay the bill and Louis, Rene, and Remy all rose to get their coats. "What shall we do with Jacques?" Louis asked.

Remy said, as he watched Jacques' head drop onto his chest, "We can't just leave him here and let the restaurant staff deal with him."

Quartermaine walked over to his colleagues, "Sacker and I will get Jacques home." Shaking each of their hands, "It has been an honour and a privilege to work with all of you once more. I hope it will not be another five years before we see each other again."

"Thank you for the wonderful meal," Remy said, gratefully.

"Oh, don't thank me," Sacker replied. "Thanks goes to our benefactor, Mister Sherlock Holmes. He doesn't know it yet, but he bought dinner for all of us tonight."

The revelation drew a hearty laugh from the group. Sacker looked over at a dozing Jacques. "Am I to assume we are taking Jacques home?"

"You and I," Quartermaine answered.

"Then I presume this is goodbye, gentlemen," Sacker said, shaking each man's hand. "I could not have chosen a better troupe of heroes with whom to fight this battle. I am in your debt, each and every one."

Once goodbyes were said and the other three colleagues had departed, Quartermaine asked the maître 'd to hail a carriage for them, while he and Sacker did their best to get Jacques to his feet, get his coat on him, and walk him out the door. When the carriage arrived, the two men hoisted their large, inebriated friend into the carriage, and climbed in. Quartermaine called up to the driver, "Ten Cavee Saint Firmin, Montreuil-sur-mer, s'il vous plait."

Nearly an hour later, the carriage pulled up in front of the home of Jacques Duquesne. Quartermaine hopped out and asked the driver to wait one moment. He ran to the door and knocked. Jacques' wife, Marie, answered. She cried out, happily, "Algernon! How good to see you. Is my husband with you?"

"He is, madame. But, I fear he has had a bit too much of his favourite burgundy this evening. My friend, Ormond, is with him in the carriage."

A look of displeasure came across Marie's face. "Bon chagrin. Que vais-je faire de lui?"

"I do not know what you can do with Jacques besides putting him to bed and letting him sleep it off. But, Marie, I would not be too harsh with him. He, and his friend Louis, saved the life of the President of France today. I think he earned his burgundy tonight."

"Mon Dieu! President Carnot? My Jacques did that?"

"He did indeed. If you don't mind, I am going to help my friend Ormond bring Jacques inside."

"Yes, yes. Of course," Marie said, holding the door open.

Quartermaine helped Sacker carry their inebriated friend into his home. "Where do you want him?"

"Put him there, on the sofa. I do not want to smell his stinking breath in my bed all night."

Sacker and Quartermaine just smiled and laid Jacques on the sofa. Marie handed Sacker a blanket and he covered his loud-snoring friend. He turned to Marie. "May I please use your washstand, madame? It seems Jacques left a little souvenir on my sleeve."

"It is the small room, second door on the left."

While Sacker was cleaning his coat sleeve and washing his hands, he noticed a small bottle of laudanum next to the basin. He made a mental note and finished cleaning up. When he rejoined Quartermaine and Marie in the living room, he paused, unsure quite how to ask his query. "Madame," he blurted, "I noticed a small vial next to the basin. I am loath to ask, but is Jacques using laudanum for any reason?"

Marie suddenly flushed with embarrassment. "Monsieur Sacker, the laudanum is not for Jacques. It is for me. My doctor prescribed laudanum for me to take at certain times when I might experience some measure of malaise."

Sacker looked at Madame Duquesne with some discomfiture. "I am sorry if I embarrassed you, Madame."

Quartermaine grabbed Sacker by the arm, "I think we are done here. Goodnight, Madame. Please tell Jacques goodbye for us." And with that, the two men exited, climbed back in the carriage, and the men were on their way back to their hotel. Quartermaine and Sacker discussed the obscurities of a woman's anatomy as his companion explained to Sacker the utility of laudanum for a woman at certain times, a thought began to formulate in his brain. When the carriage pulled up in front of Le Grand Hotel du Louvre, the two men climbed out. Quartermaine paid the driver and thanked him for his patience. As the two men entered and crossed the hotel lobby, he turned to Sacker. "I have an idea. I may have figured out a way to get Sleeves from Paris to London without being detected."

"So, what is your idea?"

"Not here. Too many ears in this lobby. Let us go up to your room and then we can discuss it."

The two men sat for more than an hour going over Quartermaine's idea. "Brilliant!" exclaimed Sacker when they were done. "Seven tomorrow morning for breakfast?"

"Done. I need to pack my things tonight if we are checking out in the morning. Do you want to take care of the carriage, or shall I?"

"I will arrange for a carriage first thing in the morning. I need to find Phillipe and thank him for everything he has done for us during our stay. I will meet you in front of the restaurant at seven."

"I will be there," Quartermaine responded, rising and heading for the door.

After Algernon exited, Sacker started to pack his things. Then it occurred to him he needed to send a telegram to Holmes to let him know they were coming back to London and had a valuable prisoner in tow. He finished packing his valise and then sat at his desk, took out pen and paper, and began drafting a cipher for Holmes. It only took him fifteen minutes to structure his missive and convert it to a cypher he knew Holmes would be able to easily translate. Then he undressed, put out the light, and went to bed. It was one in the morning. Sacker had less than six hours before he would need to be in the lobby again.

*   *   *   *   *

CHAPTER TWO

The Contemptible Mister Sleeves

In the morning, as promised, Sacker was standing in front of the lobby restaurant. Quartermaine approached. "Is everything set?"

"I found Phillipe this morning. I thanked him for his assistance and gave him twenty francs as a demonstration of our gratitude. Oh, yes, and he arranged for a carriage for us this morning. I also took care of our hotel bills. I hope you are hungry. Because I have already worked up an appetite."

"I have certainly not been as industrious as you, my friend. But I did stop at the front desk and found out where the nearest apothecary is located. Let's have breakfast and be on our way. We have much to do this morning."

The two men ordered substantial breakfast meals, since they were both quite sure it might be the only meal that they would have time for the entire day. Quartermaine also asked the waiter to bring a loaf of bread, wrapped in paper, and a bottle of wine, at the conclusion of their meal. After the two men consumed every bit of their breakfast, they paid their bill, took their parcels, and walked to the front door of the hotel, where a smiling Phillipe stood, watching over their valises. "Your carriage awaits." The young man loaded the valises of the two men into the boot of the carriage, then came around and opened the door of the carriage for them. "Where did you want to go, messieurs?"

"Twenty-two Rue Rambuteau," Quartermaine replied. Phillipe relayed that address to the driver, as Quartermaine and Sacker sat back in the carriage. Ten he poked his head in the window of the carriage one last time. "Thank you, messieurs. It has been a pleasure to be of service to you. Au revoir." Then he stepped back and the carriage pulled away.

"Twenty-two Rue Rambuteau. Is that the apothecary?"

"It is. It is the nearest apothecary to the prefecture, and we need to pick up some supplies before we meet with Henri. Do you need to stop at the telegraph office before we go to the prefecture?"

"No. I left the telegram in an envelope with Phillipe. I asked him to deliver it to the telegraph office before nine this morning. I trust he will do as I requested. He has delivered missives for me before and has never failed me."

When the carriage pulled up in front of the apothecary, the chemist was just unlocking the front door. He turned to see Quartermaine stepping down from the carriage. "I am not open yet, young man. As you can see, I have just arrived myself."

"No worries, monsieur. I can wait for you. I need only two items, which I am sure will take no time at all, once you are ready to dispense them."

As the chemist opened the door to the apothecary, he extended his arm. "After you, monsieur."

Quartermaine entered and the short, grey-haired, bespectacled chemist followed. "What may I get for you?"

"Well, when I was a soldier, I suffered an injury in battle and, every once in a while, the pain resurrects itself. The only thing that I find seems to quell the nagging pain is some laudanum mixed with my tea. My doctor also said I suffer from asthma, from years of inhaling desert dust. He prescribed chloroform to address that, but I seem to have run out. If you could replenish those items for me, I would be in your debt."

"There is no need for you to be in my debt. All you owe me is one franc, fifty centimes." The chemist walked behind the counter at the back of his shop, rummaged for a moment under the counter, and produced two small glass bottles of liquid, one of laudanum and the other of chloroform. He placed them on the counter. "I assume you know how to use these?"

"I believe so. I mix ten or twenty drops of laudanum with my tea and I should feel relief in about half an hour."

"Monsieur, if you mix twenty drops of Rousseau's laudanum with your tea, in a half hour you will feel nothing. That is three times the prescribed dose of this medicine. There are other, weaker versions of this medicine, which is what you might have been given in the past. But Rousseau's laudanum is quite potent, so be careful how you dispense it."

"Thank you for the warning. Any cautions regarding the chloroform?"

The chemist turned and opened a cabinet behind him. He withdrew a sponge and placed it on the counter. "Use this with the chloroform. Place a few drops on the sponge and then place it over your nose and breathe in deeply. That should relieve your asthma spasms for a time."

Quartermaine picked up the two bottles and the sponge and placed them in his pockets. He paid the chemist. "Merci, monsieur. You are a life saver. Au revoir." He exited the apothecary, climbed back into the carriage and knocked on the roof, calling up to the driver, "One Rue de Lutece, Place Louis Lepine, s'il vous plait."

When the carriage arrived in front of the police prefecture, the two men climbed out. The driver climbed down and unloaded their valises from the boot. Sacker paid the driver, and he and Quartermaine made their way up the stairs and entered the building. Quartermaine asked the gendarme at the desk if Prefect Loze was available. The gendarme said the prefect had been in his office since early morning and had instructed that he should not be disturbed. Quartermaine looked directly at the young man behind the desk. "We were here late last night and met with Prefect Loze. He told us to return this morning to meet with him again. Please go tell Prefect Loze that Algernon Quartermaine and Ormond Sacker have arrived. Trust me, he will want to meet with us."

The young gendarme rose from his chair and hurried down the hallway toward Loze's office. Some shouting could be heard and then it was quiet again. In a few moments, the young gendarme returned. "Prefect Loze will see you now."

Sacker and Quartermaine strode down the hallway to Loze's office. "Come in, gentlemen. After the morning I have had, it is good to see some friendly faces. Prime Minister Floquet and Chief Goron have informed me it is incumbent upon me to solve a most bizarre case of robbery at Banque de France. What news have you for me this morning?"

"More bad news, I'm afraid, Henri. It seems George Harrington Sleeves died last night from wounds suffered during his capture."

"What? How could that be? When you brought him in last night, his only injury was a broken nose. And he has been locked in solitary confinement in the barracks all night. I do not understand how this could have happened."

"Calm yourself, Henri. While we have not checked on his condition this morning, I believe Sleeves is still alive and, I am sure, still grousing in the detention cell where we left him last night. Nonetheless, he needs to be declared deceased."

Henri Loze stared blankly at the two men. Quartermaine began again. "Henri, let me ask you a question. Has the informant inside the police force been identified yet by Chief Goron?"

"He has not. And his focus has shifted away from that task for now."

"Then Sleeves needs to be declared deceased, or Sleeves, Sacker, and I will not make it out of Paris alive. If the organization he works for finds out we have him in custody, they will stop at nothing to silence him. But, if they think he is dead, they will stop searching for him. He will no longer be a threat to their identity."

"But declaring him dead will do little if one of their associates sees you and Monsieur Sacker traveling with another man. They will immediately assume it is Sleeves, will they not?"

"Not if Sacker and I leave this building in a cart with a coffin on board."

"You intend to put Sleeves in a coffin? Do you think he will just lie inside the box quietly?"

"He will, Henri. You just have to trust me."

"Do I want to know how you are going to accomplish that feat?" Then holding up his hand, Loze blurted, "Never mind, I am already sorry I asked."

"Henri, do you have anyone in the coroner's office whom you trust?"

"Jacques Duquesne's brother works in the coroner's office. He is very trustworthy."

"Do you trust him enough to stay silent about what you are going to ask him to do?"

"What *I* am going to ask him to do? Wait. What am I going to ask him to do?

"We need a certificate of death and a coffin."

"And his absolute silence on the matter," Sacker added.

 "And then what?"

"Then, Henri, a cart driver will take Sacker and I, and our dear departed Sleeves, to Gare du Nord, where we are going to take a train to Calais. From there, we are going to take a ferry to Dover, where we will transfer to a train which will take us to London. We will need about an hour with Sleeves before the coroner arrives. Do you think you can arrange to get Jacques' brother here by then?"

"I will do what I can. But I have no idea what he is going to say when I ask him to come here at a moment's notice."

"You need only tell him you have a body that needs to be examined and that a box will be needed to transport it. Tell him the rest when he arrives. If he objects to any of it when he gets here, we will have to improvise. But I trust your powers of persuasion, Henri. We will go see Monsieur Sleeves now, unless there is anything else you need from us."

"No, go, please go. I will send someone over to the coroner's office immediately."

"Would you mind if we leave our valises here while we go visit our prisoner?" Sacker asked.

"No, I do not mind. Leave them over there in the corner. They will remind me you will soon be leaving."

Quartermaine moved the valises into the corner and removed the parcel wrapped in paper and the bottle of wine. "Going away gifts for Sleeves."

As Sacker walked along to the old barracks with Quartermaine, he mused, "Did you ever notice there seems to be an inordinate amount of nepotism in the ranks in Paris?"

"You have no idea."

When the two men reached the entrance to the old barracks, Quartermaine paused. He sat at the top of the stairs leading down to the detention cells and took the laudanum bottle from his pocket. "Open the wine, Ormond."

Ormond pulled the cork from the wine bottle and held the bottle steady as Quartermaine put ten drops of laudanum in the wine. "Is that enough?"

"The chemist told me seven drops was all that was needed to relieve pain. I want to make sure Sleeves takes a good, long nap, so I think ten drops should do the trick."

Once they were sure the laudanum was settled well enough in the wine, Sacker pushed the cork back in the bottle, and the two men headed for the detention cell where they had left Sleeves the night before. As they approached, Sleeves rose from the cot and walked toward the bars. "So, you two finally came to your senses and are going to let me go?"

"Not quite, Sleeves. But we did bring you something to tide you over until the proper authorities can come to take you away." He handed the loaf of bread wrapped in paper through the bars. "Here's some fresh baked bread for you." Then he held out the bottle of wine in front of the bars. "Now, before I hand this to you, you should know, this is the only thing you are going to have to drink before they come to get you. If I hand this to you and you throw it back at us, you are not getting anything else. And then we will come in there and take the bread away as well. Do you understand?"

Sleeves thought for a moment. He looked squarely at Sacker, "I understand," he said, holding out his hand through the bars. Sacker handed Sleeves the bottle and stepped back. "Now, you understand this. When I get out of here, *and I will get out of here*, I will make it my mission to end the two of you."

Sacker looked at Quartermaine. "Are you afraid, Algie?"

"I am terrified, Ormond."

"Enjoy your breakfast. We'll check in on you and say our goodbyes before the authorities come to take you away." A tirade of curses was hurled at their backs as they walked away. When out of earshot of Sleeves, Sacker turned to Quartermaine. "How long do you think it will take?"

"It all depends on how much of the wine he drinks. In any event, I would venture to guess that in an hour or so we will have a more passive George Harrington Sleeves."

The two men made their way back to the main offices of the prefecture. As they approached the office of Prefect Henri Loze, a young gendarme intercepted them. "If you will follow me, si'l vous plait. Prefect Loze has asked me to show you to an office down the hall. He is in a meeting at present with Doctor Duquesne. He will have me fetch you when his meeting is concluded."

"Lead the way," Quartermaine responded.

The two men sat quietly for the better part of an hour. There was not much to say and, after days of frenetic goings-on, the silence was comforting and appreciated. Finally, there was a knock at the door and then the young gendarme opened the door and entered. "Pardonnez-moi, messieurs, Prefect Loze will see you now." They followed the young man back down the hall. The gendarme opened the door to the prefect's office and the two men entered. Loze was standing behind his desk and seated in front of his desk was a dark-haired man, impeccably dressed in a brown tweed suit. His strong jaw and angular nose were remarkably evocative of their colleague, Jacques. Quartermaine stepped toward the man and extended his hand in friendship. "You must be Jacques' brother."

The doctor stood, shaking hands with Quartermaine. "I am he. My name is Francois Duquesne, and I am a physician and medical examiner for this jurisdiction. And you are?"

"Algernon Quartermaine. Your brother and I have known each other for some time. We worked together at the Surete about five years ago, and we have been working together again the last few weeks. It is a pleasure to meet you at last. This is my colleague, Ormond Sacker."

Sacker stepped forward and offered his hand. "Pleasure to meet you, Doctor."

The doctor sat back down. "I understand you gentlemen have a rather unique request. You want me to provide a certificate of death, pronouncing a man deceased, without the benefit of an examination or autopsy. And you also want me to provide a box in which you will transport this *deceased man* to parts unknown. Have I left anything out?"

Sacker spoke up, "Well, Doctor, we would also appreciate some help getting the body to Gare du Nord. So, we were hoping you might have arrived here in an ambulance."

"Is there anything else?"

"No, I think that is all we need."

Before the doctor could respond, Quartermaine interjected, "I know it is a great deal to ask of you, Doctor Duquesne. You do not know us. But I hope that the trust Prefect Loze and your own brother have in us will mitigate any concerns you may have. The man we are trying to get out of the country is a merciless killer in his own right and he deserves whatever sentence will befall him in the future. But, right now, he is our only link to a criminal organization that was responsible for the foiled assassination attempts on President Carnot and Prime Minster Floquet yesterday. They are ruthless in their methods.

These men would stop at nothing to silence him if they knew he was alive. Therefore, we have devised this ruse to get him out of France. But we cannot succeed without the help of good men such as yourself."

"Can I, at least, see the man?"

Prefect Loze looked over at the doctor. "Francois, the man is locked in a detention cell in the old barracks building. These men will take you there if you feel you must see him. But, honestly, I do not know what seeing him will accomplish."

"If anyone were to ever ask me if I examined the body, I could honestly answer I had. I know it is a trifle, but I would like to maintain some semblance of believability."

"We will take you to him, Doctor," Quartermaine replied, opening the door to Loze's office.

The doctor rose from his chair. "Merci, monsieur," he said, stepping into the hallway.

The three men walked back to the old barracks. As they took the stairs down to the detention cell level, Quartermaine cautioned the doctor. "This man is a vile character, prone to epithets and threats of harm. Pay him no heed. He will be gone from France by nightfall."

"Monsieur, I was an army surgeon for two years before I took the position of medical examiner. I have heard every epithet any man could spew at me. When you are taking a man's leg or his arm, there is not much he will not say. I am sure I have heard worse than anything this man can utter. I will be fine." As they turned the corner and approached the cell where Sleeves was confined, the doctor observed Sleeves lying face down on the floor of the cell. "I think he will not have much to say at all. Open the cell door, so I can examine him." Sacker unlocked the cell door and stepped back. The doctor entered and turned Sleeves onto his back. "Can you gentlemen pick him up and put him on the cot?" he said, taking the nearly empty wine bottle from the cot. "Did you dose him with something?"

"Laudanum," Quartermaine responded, retrieving the small bottle from his coat pocket and holding it out to the doctor.

"Rousseau's laudanum. This is a potent linctus. How much did you put in the wine?"

"The chemist told me that seven drops in a cup of tea was enough to relieve pain. I thought we would need more than that in a whole bottle, so I put in ten or twelve drops."

The doctor placed his ear to Sleeves' chest and listened for a heartbeat. "Well, he is still alive. His breathing is slow and shallow, but his heartbeat is steady. He is going to be unconscious for some time."

"Have you seen everything you need to see, Doctor?" Sacker asked.

"I have, monsieur. You will find an ambulance waiting outside the rear entrance to this building. Do your best not to startle the driver. There is a stretcher in the back of the ambulance. He will help you carry this man out while I go back to Henri's office and complete the certificate of death. What is this man's name?"

"George Harrington Sleeves," Quartermaine replied. "I do not know his age, so you can choose any date you deem appropriate. I believe Prefect Loze was going to release a statement to the newspapers that all the men that died in the assassination attempts died yesterday. So, Sleeves would be included with those villains."

Sacker and the driver carried the motionless body of Sleeves to the ambulance, with Quartermaine following close behind. When the driver opened the rear door to the ambulance, Sacker noticed the back was empty, save for a small leather doctor's bag and a haversack filled with medical supplies. "Where is the coffin?"

The driver looked quizzically at Sacker. "Monsieur, we need to take this man's body to the morgue for further examination. When Doctor Duquesne is completed with his autopsy, we will prepare the body for burial. At that time, he will be placed in a coffin."

"Autopsy?"

"Certainement. We will take him to the morgue at Hotel-Dieu and the doctor will complete his examination there."

"I see, " was all Sacker could muster. Quartermaine stepped over to his colleague and whispered. "It appears the doctor has not confided in anyone, Ormond. We will just have to play along for the time being."

The doctor finally appeared at the same rear door through which they had brought Sleeves' unconscious body to the ambulance. "I will ride up top with the driver. You can ride back here with your prisoner. It is a short ride to Hotel-Dieu. I trust you will not be too uncomfortable."

When the doctor closed the rear door to the ambulance, Sacker looked across at Quartermaine. "I am beginning to think that doctor does not like us."

"I do not think it is personal, Ormond. I just think he does not appreciate the position we have put him in. If he is anything like his brother, Jacques, he is an honorable man, and we have asked him to do something that does not sit well with his sense of right and wrong. All the same, he has agreed, and for that we should be thankful."

The ambulance pulled up to the rear entrance to Hotel-Dieu. The driver hopped down from his seat and took a tether-weight from beneath the carriage. He attached it to the bridle of the horse, then went around to the rear of the ambulance and opened the door. "Messieurs, we are at the hospital. Do you need assistance carrying the body inside?"

"We will be fine. We can carry this fellow in," Quartermaine replied.

The doctor came around the side of the ambulance. "Shall we proceed, gentlemen?" The doctor led the men down a flight of steps and along a dimly lit corridor. There was the unmistakable smell of death as they approached the morgue. The doctor opened the door, and the two men carried the stretcher over to a table on which they placed the body of Sleeves. The doctor turned up the gas lamps to provide a good deal more light. "We will need to move quickly, gentlemen. Henri told me he was going to inform the newspapers of the death of the assassins this morning. By this afternoon, the papers will be splashing the news on every corner in Paris. Shortly after, there will be crowds of people at the Paris Morgue, hoping to catch a glimpse of the villains."

"What are you saying? Sacker asked, unawares.

"If this man is as wanted as you claim, when his body is not on display at the Paris Morgue, those looking to be sure he is dead are going to question where he is. They may even presume he is not dead at all, and on the run. Whatever you are going to do with this man, you need to do it quickly. There is a side room over there," he said, pointing to a worn and battered door. "You will find three empty coffins in there. Let us get this man inside one of them and get him out of here. I do not wish to put anyone in this hospital at risk."

The two men retrieved a wooden box from the room and brought it back, setting it next to the table where Sleeves' body lie. They picked him up and set him down inside the box. Sacker went back to the room and retrieved a small toolbox, containing nails and a ball-peen hammer. As he placed the lid on the coffin, he looked up. "I am curious, doctor. How long can a man survive inside a closed coffin?"

Doctor Duquesne stepped over to the coffin and looked down at Sleeves. "I would presume, by his height and weight, his body volume is approximately seventy liters. If my estimate is correct, roughly eight hundred liters of air, of which approximately one hundred sixty liters is oxygen, would remain once the lid is closed. He is unconscious, so his breathing will be slow. Assuming he remains unconscious, he should consume less than a liter of air per hour. I would venture to say he will have four to five hours of air before you will need to open the box."

Sacker thought for a moment. Then he took the ball-peen hammer from the toolbox and, with one good whack, knocked a hole the size of a twenty franc coin in the end of the coffin.

"What was that for?" Quartermaine asked.

"Just in case we can't open this box in four hours," Sacker said, fastening the lid atop the coffin with six nails. When he was finished, Sacker looked up. "That should do the trick. Doctor, we are ready to go. Is there any chance your driver could take us to Gare du Nord? We still have time to catch the one-thirty train to Calais if we can get there in the next half hour."

"I have already given him instructions to do so. The ambulance is waiting outside the same door where we entered." He retrieved the death certificate from his inside coat pocket and handed it to Quartermaine. "I believe you will be needing this document, monsieur."

"We cannot thank you enough, Doctor." The two men carried the coffin containing the unconscious body of Sleeves to the ambulance. They loaded the coffin inside and climbed aboard. The driver slammed the door shut, climbed up into his seat, and snapped the reins. The ambulance lurched forward. When they arrived at the train station, the driver hopped down and went around to the back and opened the door. Quartermaine asked the driver to stay with the ambulance while he went to purchase tickets and a baggage pass. The driver agreed and Quartermaine made his way to the ticket window. Sacker sat quietly in the back of the ambulance next to the coffin. The driver took advantage of the silence and smoked a cigarette while he waited. When Quartermaine returned, he asked the driver to pull the ambulance up to the baggage car so they could load the coffin onto the train. When that task was accomplished, Quartermaine shook the driver's hand and gave him a ten franc gold coin for his assistance. "Nous ne saurions trop vous remercier, monsieur, vous nous avez beaucoup aides. Nous vous sommes redevables."

The driver tipped his cap, "Au revoir, messieurs," he said, as he strode toward the front of the ambulance and climbed aboard. He drove off, leaving Quartermaine and Sacker to their own devices. As the two men stood outside the baggage car, Sacker said, "One of us should stay back here with the coffin, just in case our guest happens to wake up."

"Not sure that is allowed. We will need to check with the conductor."

"Why would they not let a grieving sibling stay with his dear, recently departed brother?"

"'I am not sure if that ruse will work. But we can give it a try." The two men approached the conductor, Quartermaine, his arm around Sacker's shoulder, consoling him. After a few minutes of theatrics and cajoling, the conductor relented and allowed Sacker to ride in the baggage car alongside the coffin, with one caveat. "You must agree you will not hold the company responsible for any injury you may incur if you are jostled about if the train has to stop suddenly."

"Understood," said Sacker, climbing aboard.

"I will be in the next car forward," Quartermaine advised. "I will see you in Calais."

As Quartermaine came down the ramp of the baggage car, he noticed two men standing next to one of the ceiling support-beams near the empty track across from the Paris-to-Calais train. As he glanced over to size them up, they both turned their faces away, then slowly walked back toward the station. Quartermaine thought to follow them, but the conductor called out a final notice to board, so he moved quickly to the steps to the passenger car directly in front of the baggage car and boarded the train. Once inside, he found a seat near the window and kept a lookout for the two men. As he glanced out the window, he saw the two men dashing past, running for all they were worth for the next car ahead, as the train lurched forward and began to pull out of Gare du Nord station.

The train ride was unusually quiet, almost too quiet for Quartermaine's liking. There were but a few passengers sitting forward of Quartermaine in the last passenger car on the train. There were three men, each in his own seat, quietly reading the morning newspaper. On the opposite side of the car, halfway up the aisle, there was a young couple. The young woman was seated by the window and would occasionally turn excitedly to her beau, pointing out something she had just seen as the train rolled along. Sitting quietly alone, Quartermaine felt a restlessness after everything that had transpired in the days previous. His mind wandered, as he stared out the window, watching the scenery fly by. He sat undisturbed with his thoughts for more than an hour, when, as the train passed through Amiens, the door at the far end of the passenger car opened, and the two men Quartermaine had observed in Gare du Nord entered and walked toward the back of the car. They walked past Quartermaine, paying him no heed, and opened the door behind him. They stepped through and closed the door, crossing over to the baggage car. One of the men opened the baggage car door and stepped through, the second man following close behind. Sacker, somewhat startled, stood up. "I don't think you men are supposed to be in here."

"What are *you* doing in here, then?"

"I am accompanying my brother's body to Le Touquet, where I am going to bury him next to our parents. I was given permission to be here by the conductor. I think you should leave."

"And I think you are lying, monsieur. We know who you are, Monsieur Sacker. Our employer sent us to find you and bring you back to Paris to explain what has happened to Monsieur Sleeves."

"I think you have me confused with someone else. I came to Paris to claim the body of my brother, and I am bringing him back to Le Touquet to be buried in the family plot."

"You speak English remarkably well for a peasant from Le Touquet," the large man replied, drawing a pistol from his belt. "And it seems your English is better than your memory, Monsieur Sacker. My memory, however, does not suffer from that same deficit. I remember your face.

You and I shared a jail cell in Berlin for a night not so long ago. You were arrested with the rest of us when the Kriminalpolizei stormed into the Ratskellar in Copenick and dragged us all away. I also remember that, by some strange chance, you were released that same night. So, either you have friends in high places, or…you are a spy. If I did not have instructions to bring you back to Paris, I would kill you right here, and be done with it."

40

Sacker stood up, his hands in the air. "It seems you have me at a disadvantage, gentlemen. However, you should know I do not know what happened to Monsieur Sleeves. It is possible he has run off as he did in Copenick that night. You think me a spy, but I went to jail with the rest of you. Sleeves did not suffer that same fate since he disappeared in all the confusion. I tracked him to Paris and was working with him on the assassination plots. When everything went into a cocked hat, he was nowhere to be found – again. I got on this train to get to Calais so as to escape to England. That is the whole of it."

"That is not quite the whole of it, monsieur. We have orders to bring you back to Paris, and that is what we are going to do."

Suddenly, the door to the baggage car opened and Algernon Quartermaine stepped in, pistol drawn and leveled in the direction of the two men. He stepped forward quickly and pressed the barrel of his weapon against the skull of the larger man. "Carefully lower your weapon, sir."

"I think not. I have my pistol trained on Monsieur Sacker and if I cannot take him back to Paris with me, I will kill him here." He began to cock his revolver when a sharp blow to the back of his head felled him instantly. The smaller man leapt for the gun as it hit the floor. Sacker took one step forward, placing his foot over the weapon. As the small man looked up, he saw Sacker's fist crashing down toward his face. He did not have time to duck away and took the punch squarely on his jaw. He fell, face-first, onto the plank floor of the baggage car.

"Two questions," Sacker began, as he checked to see if the small man were unconscious. "What do we do with these two?"

"Well, look about. There must be something we can use to tie them with," he said, starting to look about the baggage car himself. "What was your second question?"

"What took you so long?"

"I saw these two ne'er-do-wells in Gare du Nord. They were eyeing the baggage car as we were loading the coffin aboard. I didn't think much of it at the time. But when I saw them again on the train, headed for the baggage car, in truth, I thought they were simply thieves looking to do some undisturbed pilfering before the train got to Calais. I thought when they saw you in there, they would think better of their plan and turn around. It did not occur to me that these men would be after you. When they didn't come right back out, I thought it was time to see what was going on. When I got to the door, I could hear this big bloke telling you what for, and that is when I came in with my pistol at the ready."

"And none too soon, I might add. Ah ha!" he exclaimed, as he opened a small wooden bin attached to the wall of the car. Inside there was an assortment of tools and other trappings of the railway trade; signal flags, a kerosene lamp, a pry bar, a hammer, a jack-knife, and a large spool of hemp rope. Sacker unraveled about two meters of the hemp rope and cut it with the jack-knife. He made one more cut, after measuring out the rope into two equal lengths. He handed one length to Quartermaine to tie up the large fellow and kept the other to tie up the smaller man.

"Use the rope to tie his hands," Quartermaine said, pulling the large man's hands behind his back.

"Tie them tightly behind his back. We will use their belts to secure their feet."

Once the two men were securely bound, Quartermaine and Sacker dragged their still unconscious bodies into the farthest corner of the baggage car. "They are going to make a racket when they awaken," Sacker noted.

"I think not." Quartermaine reached into his pocket and withdrew the bottle of chloroform. "Can I have your handkerchief?"

Sacker withdrew his handkerchief from his coat pocket and handed it to Quartermaine. "Thank you. While I am taking care of this, can you see if there is something in that bin we could use to fashion a couple of gags?"

Sacker returned to the bin and removed the red cloth from one of the signal flags. "This should do," he said. He tore the cloth into two strips. He walked over to where Quartermaine was at work and knelt down. As he began to tie a gag across the mouth of the smaller man, there was a sudden reaction. The small man had awakened with a start, and he wagged his head back-and-forth violently to stifle Sacker's efforts. Sacker finally got the gag tied about the smaller man's mouth, but his muffled cries were still audible. Quartermaine leaned over and placed Sacker's handkerchief over the small man's nose. "Breathe in. That's right. Nice deep breath." In moments, the small man was unconscious again.

They waited for the large man to come awake, then the same procedure was performed on him. First the gag was placed over his mouth, then Quartermaine applied the handkerchief doused with a few drops of chloroform over his nose. Both men were soon lying still. The small man was breathing deeply. The large man was slumped over, an occasional muted snore punctuating his snuffling.

"That should keep them insensible until we get to Calais. When we arrive, I will find a local constable and explain we found two men trying to rob the train and did our best to restrain them. If he asks any questions, I will tell him I am working undercover for the Surete and am not at liberty to say anything more. In the meantime, can you please purchase our tickets for the ferry and arrange to have the coffin transferred from the train to the boat?"

"I will do that. I just hope it does not take much time. I do not want to leave our cargo unattended for very long. I don't know how we would explain things if he wakes while I am away."

"He should sleep soundly for another two hours or more. He drank that entire bottle of wine and there was enough laudanum in it to render a horse insensible. It would not surprise me if he slept until we reached Dover. Since there is nothing more to do here, I am going to return to my seat in the coach. I will see you in the station at Calais."

"Ta," replied Sacker, returning to the bench attached to the baggage car wall.

*   *   *   *   *

CHAPTER THREE

Nicking Away

When the train arrived at the Gare de Ville station in Calais, Quartermaine was quick to disembark. He walked through the station and spied a middle-aged, portly gendarme slowly pacing about near the entrance. He strode up to the gendarme and explained the situation in the baggage car. Taken aback at first, and somewhat unnerved, the gendarme seemed to not know what to do. Quartermaine asked him if there were any other policemen in the station. The gendarme raised his whistle to his lips, but Quartermaine stifled him. "Possibly we could find another policeman to assist, without raising an alarm, monsieur."

"Oui, that is a good thought. Come with me." He led Quartermaine toward a small office across the main lobby, where another gendarme sat quietly reading a newspaper. "Tell this officer what you told me, s'il vous plait." Quartermaine recounted the tale again and he, with the two officers in tow, made his way back to the baggage car. When they arrived, Sacker was chatting with a porter, requesting a cart to carry the coffin from the station to the ferry dock. As the two gendarmes stood peering into the baggage car, Sacker pointed to the far corner, where the two brigands were trussed up, still unconscious. Seeing the two men, the portly gendarme turned to Quartermaine. "Are they dead?"

"No, monsieur. They are merely unconscious. It happened during our scuffle with them. If there is nothing more you need from us, we will be on our way. We have a ferry to catch to take us to Dover," Quartermaine replied, stepping next to the coffin as it was being removed from the baggage car. "And my friend and I have a fallen comrade here whom we are taking to be buried in his family's plot outside of Croydon. So, if you will excuse us…"

"I do have a few more questions," said the second gendarme. "It will only take a few moments."

Quartermaine stepped closer to the gendarme. "If we could step over here, monsieur," he said, escorting the gendarme by the arm away from the others. He lowered his voice and whispered to the gendarme, "Monsieur, my name is Algernon Quartermaine. I am working undercover for the Surete. My immediate superior is Henri Loze, the Prefect of Police in Paris. He reports directly to the Chief of the Surete, Marie-Francois Goron. I cannot divulge to you the details of my work, but I assure you it is of the utmost importance. So, unless you wish to incur the wrath of Chief Goron, I would suggest you take the two unconscious men in the baggage car into custody and allow my friend and I to be on our way."

"Pardonnez-moi, monsieur. How was I to know such things? We will take those men into custody. But, may I ask, what are we to charge them with?"

Quartermaine thought for a moment, then replied quietly, "Well, for starters, attempted robbery. But, if you are willing to be somewhat industrious, you could hold them over for the attempted assassination of Kaiser Wilhelm in Germany. I am sure the Kriminalpolizei would be most grateful for your cooperation." Quartermaine patted the gendarme on the shoulder. "Of course, I will leave that to your good judgement." He walked back toward Sacker. "Everything has been taken care of here, Ormond. So, if you will accompany our cargo to the dock, I will go to the ticket window and secure passage on the ferry."

"Do you have the medicine? I am feeling a bit peaked, and I may suddenly feel need of it."

Quartermaine reached into his coat pocket and retrieved the bottle of chloroform and the handkerchief he had used to dose the two brigands. "Of course, brother, just be mindful of what the doctor advised. Use it sparingly."

"I will be sure to be careful," Sacker replied, climbing aboard the horse-cart which bore the coffin. "I will catch you up."

As dusk began to fall, the steam packet Invicta, the last ferry of the day from Calais, cleared the dock. Quartermaine found the compartment assigned to himself and Sacker but had not seen his colleague since the porters had loaded the coffin onto the lower deck. Sacker had given the porters five francs each to allow him to follow them to wherever it was they were going to store the coffin. After a quarter hour had passed, Sacker finally appeared at the compartment door. He entered, sat down across from Quartermaine, and returned the bottle of chloroform to his colleague.

"Where have you been?"

"I was worried that our traveling companion might wake on the way to Dover, so I gave him a few sniffs from the handkerchief. He should sleep like a baby."

"How in the world did you get the coffin opened?"

Sacker reached into his coat pocket and, to Quartermaine's amazement, retrieved a small pry bar. "I filched this from the bin on the baggage car. I thought it might come in handy if we needed to open the box for any reason."

"Brilliant! But didn't the porters see you open the box?"

"The porters loaded everything from the dock onto the boat and then returned to the dock. No one ever questioned why I remained by the coffin. I suppose they thought I was just paying my last respects. In any event, I was alone when I gave our man Sleeves a few sniffs from the handkerchief. When I finished, I replaced the lid to the coffin and nailed it shut again. Then I came up here to find you. I finally feel we can settle for a bit, at least until we get to Dover. Shall we get a drink? I happen to know this boat has a first-class saloon."

Peering out the window of the aft saloon at the churning Channel waters, Quartermaine's thoughts wandered a bit. Sacker noticed his friend and colleague deep in thought and brought a second glass of sherry over to him. "What has you so deep in thought, my friend?"

"Have you given any thought to what we will do after this whole escapade is concluded?"

"You mean if we live to tell of it?"

"I'm being serious, Ormond. Have you thought at all about what comes next?"

"I suppose I will go back to what I was doing before Sherlock Holmes contacted me for this adventure. I will manage the family estate, as I have done since my father's passing. I have an apartment in London, but I also own the manor house, which I inherited, and there are tenant farms on our land, from which I receive an income. I also have invested money in coal mines owned by Wentworth-Fitzwilliam. It is a comfortable life, to be sure, even if it is a bit humdrum. It certainly is not as engaging as your life. As I understand it, you are an assistant to Howard Vincent, a member of Parliament. That must keep you in the thick of things."

"It is not as glamorous or as thrilling as you may think, Ormond. I am not much more than an overvalued secretary. I manage the MP's schedule, transcribe his correspondence, and do a hundred other menial jobs for the MP. It is not challenging in the least, and I dread the thought of returning to that mundane existence." He downed his glass of sherry. "Don't they have a good ale in this saloon?"

"I will get us each an ale, Algernon, if that will cheer your spirits." Sacker went to the bar and returned with two pints of Bass Pale Ale. "So, tell me, my friend, what is it you would rather do?"

"As insane as this may sound, I would rather be doing what we are doing now. These past few weeks, I have never felt more useful and alive. I envy your friend Sherlock Holmes. His life must be extraordinary."

"You have no idea."

"I actually do have an idea. And I do not expect you to reply upon hearing it. But, I would ask you to consider what I am about to propose. Ormond, would you consider going into business together in the same line of business as your friend, Sherlock Holmes?"

"As consulting detectives? Seriously?"

"Yes. What say you?"

"I say…I need to think it over. You caught me a bit off guard, my friend. I'll need some time to consider it."

"I understand. But I think we make a brilliant team. So, please, promise me you will give it some serious consideration."

"I will, I promise," Sacker replied, draining his pint of ale.

The Invicta arrived in Dover shortly after six in the evening. Quartermaine and Sacker retrieved their valises from the overhead netting, left their compartment, and proceeded to the dock. Quartermaine headed to the train station to purchase tickets on the first train to London. Sacker proceeded to the dock to await the unloading of the coffin. As he stood, watching the porters offload the various packages, bales, and crates, he heard a faint, familiar voice behind him. "Two shillings to carry your bag for you, sir," came the offer.

Sacker smiled and turned about, holding out his valise. "Well, that is a right fair price for such a job, Master Devon Lancaster."

The boy's face lit up with delight as he recognized Ormond's face immediately. "Blimey, sir. I am glad to see you back on English soil."

"And I am glad to be back, young squire. But why are you not home having your dinner?"

"Last boat of the day, sir. I was hoping to make a few shillings before I went home. I am glad you are my last patron of the night."

"Well, instead of a few shillings how would you like to earn yourself a gold sovereign?" Sacker asked, bending down to be face-to-face with the boy.

"Would I ever. What do you need me to do, sir?"

"I have a box coming off the Invicta, and I need to get it onto the train to London. Do you think you could find a porter with a cart and bring him back here to get that done?"

"I can and I will. Whoosh!" he exclaimed, as he ran off in the direction of the train station. By the time Devon Lancaster arrived back at the dock with a porter and baggage cart in tow, the coffin was lying on the dock at Sacker's feet. The boy stared at the coffin and then looked up at Sacker. "You didn't tell me it was a coffin, sir."

"Would it have made any difference, Master Lancaster?"

"No, sir, I suppose not."

Sacker asked the porter to help him lift the coffin onto the cart. He handed the porter five shillings. "Will you please take this to the baggage car and wait there for me? I need to get a baggage tag for the box to be loaded aboard the train." He looked at Devon Lancaster. "Young squire, will you go with the porter and keep an eye on the coffin for me? I will return as soon as I find my friend."

The porter and the boy headed off toward the train shed at the Dover terminus and Sacker headed to the station, in search of Quartermaine. The two men connected in the lobby. "The train leaves in twenty minutes from track number three." He handed Sacker his ticket and a tag for the coffin. "I will meet you on board, Ormond. I will sit in the first Pullman car directly in front of the baggage car." As they came to the baggage car, Quartermaine proceeded on to the Pullman cars. Sacker walked over to the conductor and handed him the tag for the coffin. The conductor motioned for the porter and the baggage handler to load the coffin aboard the train. While the two men went about their work, Sacker turned to Devon Lancaster. "You didn't hear the man inside saying anything on the way over here, did you?"

The boy looked at Sacker queerly, then slowly smiled. "Oh, sir, you're pulling my leg. A dead man can't say anything."

"Right you are, Master Devon Lancaster. Right you are." Sacker handed the boy a gold sovereign. "Now, you have earned a good day's wages. I want you to go home straightway and have your dinner. And, young man, take care of yourself."

"Thank you, sir. You do the same." The young boy waved, ran up the roadway away from the station, and disappeared into the darkness.

Sacker turned, checked once more to make sure the coffin was aboard the train, and then strode toward the Pullman.

At precisely seven o'clock, the Jupiter train to London pulled out of the Dover terminus, carrying seventy-two passengers, fourteen crates of tea leaves, twelve bales of cotton, ten trunks full of various fabrics and leather, and one coffin, containing a slumbering George Harrington Sleeves. Barring any delays or unscheduled stops, the trip to London would take approximately two and one quarter hours. Sacker found Quartermaine, comfortably situated precisely where he had explained he would be, seated in the Pullman directly in front of the baggage car. Sacker took his place across from Quartermaine, and the two gentlemen sat quietly, each contemplating what they had discussed aboard the Invicta.

*   *   *   *   *

An announcement rang out through the main concourse of Victoria Station at nine o'clock, as a porter traversed the spacious concourse, bellowing through a megaphone that the Jupiter train was arriving on Track Number Eight. In the center of the concourse, a man and two young street urchins stood patiently awaiting the arrival of the passengers from the Jupiter train. Finally, Wiggins turned to Jonah Burke. "Mister Burke, don't ya fink we should go to meet them as they get off the train?"

"I have never met these men, Wiggins. I would not know them if they walked right up to me."

"That is why Mister 'olmes sent Simpson an' me along. Simpson knows Mr. Sacker and could pick him out of a crowd. Oy really fink we should go fetch 'em, Mr. Burke."

"Tell you what, Wiggins. You go tell Mr. Hobbs the train has arrived. I will go with Simpson and
collect Sacker and Quartermaine."

"Right-o, Mr. Burke," said Wiggins, as he turned and ran off toward the main entrance on Victoria Street.

Burke looked at the dark-haired little street urchin standing at his side. "Well, don't just stand there, Simpson. Find Mr. Sacker for me."

The boy took off running, and Burke did his best to keep sight of the lad, who was ducking and bobbing between the passengers headed toward the main concourse. When he finally caught up with the lad, he was standing right in front of Ormond Sacker. "Mr. Sacker, I presume?"

"I am he. And who might you be?"

"Jonah Burke, sir. I am in the employ of Mycroft Holmes. His brother, your friend Sherlock, asked me to come and collect you and your colleague, and bring the pair of you, and any baggage you may have brought with you, to a location which would be safe from prying eyes."

"Why didn't Sherlock come to meet us himself?"

"He had business with his brother and the prime minister. They are meeting at the PM's office, and Mr. Holmes was unsure how long he would be otherwise engaged. So, he asked me and my colleague to meet you here."

"It's all right, Mr. Sacker," Simpson remarked. "These blokes are good eggs. They been workin' for Mister 'olmes for some time now. You can trust 'em."

"On your word, Simpson, I will trust them." At that moment, Quartermaine came down the steps of the Pullman car. "This is my colleague, Algernon Quartermaine."

Burke and Quartermaine shook hands. "We have a carriage of sorts waiting out front. My colleague is tending it. I was told you had another piece of baggage to transport."

"I wouldn't exactly call it baggage," said Sacker. "We have a coffin to transport. If you could follow us to the baggage car, we could collect it. Since there may be people looking for the two of us, it would be preferrable to spend as little time as possible in the train station. Could you help us carry it?"

"Of course, but we do not want to walk out the front entrance carrying a coffin. That will attract far too much attention. There is another exit that will have little or no traffic." Burke turned to Simpson. "Lad, run, fast as you can, and tell Mr. Hobbs to take the Black Maria around to the Wilton Road entrance. Tell him we will be there shortly."

Simpson ran off. Burke followed Sacker and Quartermaine to the baggage car. Porters were offloading the baggage and sundry crates and bales. The coffin was still inside the car. Sacker walked over to one of the porters, gave him five shillings, and asked he and another porter to bring the coffin to the lip of the door. As the porters pushed the coffin to the open door, Sacker and Quartermaine took hold of either side and gently lifted it down. Burke led them to a ramp which led to a long corridor, at the end of which was a large oaken door. Burke slid the door open, and the two men carried the coffin out of the station, along a cobblestone pathway, to the Black Maria, which was waiting at the curb. They loaded the coffin into the back of the wagon and climbed in on either side. Burke helped the two young boys into the back, and they found seats on either side next to the two men. "I am going to sit up top with my colleague. It is not a long ride, and we will do our best to make it steady as possible." He closed the door tight. In a few moments, there was the crack of a whip, and the carriage pitched forward.

"Ever been in one of these buggies before, Mr. Sacker?" Simpson asked.

"Can't say that I have. Why, have you?"

"Oy 'ave. Some ol' mutton shunter from Scotland Yard, name Lestrade, nabbed me for filching an ol' lady's purse. 'e tossed me into one of these buggies, and there oy was, stuck inside with this raggedy ol' codger, who sat across from me, quiet as a church-mouse 'e was. Then, just before we get to the Yard, the ol' codger takes off 'is 'at, rips off this grey mop of a wig, pulls off 'is beard and 'is nose, and who do you fink is sittin' 'cross from me? None uvver than Mr. Sherlock 'olmes 'imself. Oy was downright gobsmacked oy was. When Lestrade opened the door to the wagon, Mister 'olmes climbed out and thanked Lestrade for the ride. Then 'e told 'im oy was one of 'is Irregulars and 'e would see to it oy was looked after. Lestrade let me go straight away. An' oy've been doin' odd jobs for Mister 'olmes ever since."

"Sounds like a great stroke of luck there, Simpson."

"Luckiest day of my 'ole life, oy'd say. Uvverwise, oy'd likely be in some orphanage, doin' 'ard labour under the watchful eye of some ol' biddy."

Sacker and Quartermaine both smiled, clearly amused by the young lad's tale. Wiggins sat quietly next to Sacker, peering through the barred window across from him. "Almost there," he remarked.

When the Black Maria finally came to a stop, Burke hopped down and went around to the back of the carriage and opened the door. Wiggins and Simpson hopped out first. As Quartermaine started to climb out, he noticed another man walking briskly toward the carriage house doors. As the doors were closed, the man headed back toward the group, and as he strode up to them, Burke offered an introduction. "Let me introduce our driver, my colleague and close friend, Nathaniel Hobbs."

Then, another, more familiar voice could be heard. "I do not think I will need any introduction, gentlemen," said John Watson as he approached. "Ormond, Algernon, it is good to see you back home, safe and sound."

"For the moment, at least, Doctor," Sacker replied. "It seems that we are being pursued."

"By whom?"

"We do not know by whom, nor how many there may be. We had a situation on the train to Calais, which, thanks to my colleague, came to a satisfactory resolution. But, in truth, I have had a suspicion that we may have yet been followed to England."

"Well, you are in safe hands now. And, if I am not mistaken, we have some work ahead of us this evening. But before we begin, I must ask, what are we to do with these two ragamuffins?"

Turning to Wiggins and Simpson, Sacker drew two half-sovereigns from his pocket. "Boys, your work is done for this evening. Here is a half-sovereign for each of you, with our thanks." Then he gave Wiggins another five shillings. "Take a hansom cab and get home safe. I would rue the day I had to inform Sherlock Holmes that I lost his two best Irregulars." The two boys scampered toward the door and were gone. Sacker turned back to Watson. "If you don't mind me asking, Doctor, where is Sherlock? I expected him to meet us here tonight."

"He is otherwise occupied. He was called to 10 Downing Street this morning, along with his brother Mycroft. It had something to do with the explosion at the Bank of England when we were in Portsmouth protecting the Queen."

"Do you know what date that was, Doctor?" Quartermaine asked anxiously.

"I believe it was on the twelfth of October. As I say, it was when we were all in Portsmouth defending the Queen."

"Strange that…That was the same day we were stopping the assassinations in Paris, Ormond. And the next day, when we went to see Henri Loze, he said he had been in a meeting that morning with Chief Goron and the prime minister about an explosion at Banque de France. That seems more than a little coincidental."

"I would agree. Besides, in the main, I do not believe in coincidences. More to the point, look at the facts. Two attacks on heads of state on the same day, and on that very same day, two of the largest banks in the world suffer explosions. That is not coincidence, my friend. I would venture to say, the events were planned to occur simultaneously."

"So what do we do now?"

"I think we need to wake up George Harrington Sleeves and ask him some questions."

"That is why I was sent here to meet you," Watson said. "But I do not see the man Holmes asked me to examine."

"Oh, that. One moment, Doctor. Algernon, a little help, if you don't mind."

Quartermaine and Sacker climbed back into the Black Maria and slid the coffin to the end of the wagon. "Gentlemen, if you could assist, please."

The four men lifted the coffin out of the carriage and moved it across to a grain bin, where they set it down. Sacker withdrew the pry bar from his coat once again and opened the lid. Watson stood, his mouth agape. "Holmes told me to come examine a man. He did not tell me I would be examining a dead man."

"I certainly hope he is not dead, Doctor," said Sacker. "We have gone to great pains to get him here in one piece, alive, albeit somewhat insensible."

"How long has he been in this box?"

"We put him in the box around one this afternoon."

"So, he has been in this box for more than eight hours?"

"More or less, Doctor. The top has not been on the box the entire time. And I did knock a hole in the bottom so there was air for him to breathe."

"Then why is he still unconscious?"

"Well, you see, Doctor, he drank an entire bottle of wine, which was dosed with Rousseau's laudanum, and that seemed to put him to sleep initially. Then before we got on the steam packet to Dover, Sacker opened the up the box and gave him a few whiffs of this chloroform," Quartermaine said, handing the bottle to Watson. "He hasn't stirred the whole trip."

Watson set down his bag and took out his stethoscope. He listened for a heartbeat. After a few tense moments, he turned to Sacker and Quartermaine. "It is a miracle, but somehow this man is still alive. What condition he will be in when I awaken him, I cannot say." He reached into his bag and withdrew a small bottle of smelling salts. He placed it under Sleeves' nose and moved it back and forth slowly under his nostrils. There were a few spastic twitchings of arms and legs, then Sleeves' eyes fluttered open. Then, there was another sudden jerk as Sleeves tried to sit up. Watson pressed his hand against Sleeves' chest and restrained him. "Easy. You need to stay still. You have been unconscious for some time."

The cobwebs in Sleeves' brain slowly dissipated and his senses gradually returned to him. "Where am I?"

"Hello, Sleeves, old man," Sacker said, smiling down at Sleeves, who was still lying inside the coffin. "Like your new accommodations?"

Sleeves sat up and, realizing his current circumstance, he barked, "What in bloody hell am I doing in this coffin?"

"Just wanted you to get used to where you will be spending the rest of eternity after you are tried and hanged for treason."

"I will never go to trial. The organization I work for will see to it I walk free."

"Really?" Quartermaine inquired. "According to a report supplied by the Paris Prefect of Police to *Le Petit Journal*, you were killed attempting to flee Paris after failed assassination attempts against the President of France and his prime minister. So, not only will they not be coming to your rescue, they are not even looking for you. In fact, they have probably already replaced you."

"You are lying."

"Even if that were true, Sleeves, old man, no one will find you where you are now," Sacker responded.

"And where is that?" Sleeves enquired, looking about furtively for any clues to his whereabouts.

"In a carriage house in the south of France, where you have been brought to answer some questions about that organization you were so keen on a few moments ago," Quartermaine replied.

As Sleeves clambered out of the coffin, Burke and Hobbs both drew their revolvers. Once on the ground, Sleeves stood unsteadily, leaning against the grain bin. He glared at Quartermaine. "The organization I work for prizes its anonymity above all else. If I tell you anything, I would be a dead man."

"You silly man, according to anyone outside this carriage house, you are already a dead man," Sacker replied cynically.

"I have only your word on that."

"And that will have to be enough for now. As soon as we can get our hands on a newspaper, we will prove what we are telling you is true. Unfortunately, we did not have time when we were leaving Paris to stop for a paper. But we will see what we can do tomorrow. For now, I need you to turn around and put your hands behind your back."

When Sleeves turned around, Burke handcuffed him. Then Hobbs knelt down and placed shackles about Sleeves' ankles. "All right, you can turn back around now," Sacker said. "Sorry for the restraints, but we don't want you to get any ideas about trying to leave our cozy little carriage house."

Watson brought a stool over and set it next to Sleeves. "You have been unconscious for a good long time today. I think it best if you sit down."

Sleeves kicked the stool away. "I don't care what you think. I'll stand, if it's all the same to you."

Watson looked sternly at Sleeves. "Then I don't suppose you want anything to eat or drink either?"

The look on Sleeves' face suddenly changed. "I am parched."

Watson walked over and picked up the stool and set it back down by Sleeves. Then he walked over to a table near the horse stalls where he had laid a haversack, in which there were sandwiches, made of thick-cut wheat bread with salted ham and cress, wrapped in paper, bottles of ale and ginger beer, and a cheesecloth filled with fruit turnovers. There was also a canteen of water. He picked up the canteen and brought it over to Sleeves, who sat down silently on the stool. Watson removed the cap from the canteen and raised it to Sleeves' lips. He drank rapaciously.

"Doctor, if you could keep an eye on Mr. Sleeves for a moment, I would like to have a word with the others," Sacker said.

"We're fine here," Watson answered, replacing the cap on the canteen.

Sacker walked over to the other three men. "I did not expect that we would be here without Holmes. We are going to have to hold Sleeves here until he arrives. Any suggestions, gentlemen?"

Hobbs spoke up. "There is a groomsman's shack at the back of the carriage house. It has a parlor stove, a cot, and only one door. We could take shifts watching him. That should suffice until Holmes arrives."

Sacker called over to Watson. "Doctor, do you have any notion how long it will be before your colleague arrives?"

"I truly have no idea. But he has been gone since early morning. I cannot imagine what would be so earth-shattering that would take him twelve hours to discuss."

"I can think of a few things, Doctor," Quartermaine replied. "My only hope is what he is discussing has nothing to do with any of those things."

"Well, let us not speculate. I am sure, when he arrives, he will provide some explanation," Sacker said. "In the meantime, let us get our guest to his new accommodations. Which of you wants first shift?"

Burke piped up. "I will take first watch. What say you, two hours per shift?"

Sacker and Quartermaine nodded. "That's fine with me," Hobbs replied. "Just don't forget about Boomer."

"How could I forget? I just thought I would keep it as a surprise for our new guest," Burke responded, with a smile.

"Who or what is Boomer?" Sacker asked, curiously.

"I'll show you," Hobbs said, as he walked briskly toward the back entrance to the carriage house. He disappeared for a moment. Then the door opened again and in bounded a huge, brindle-colored bull mastiff. He covered the ground between the door and the three men in a trice, stopped at Burke's side, and sat. "This is Boomer," Hobbs said, rejoining the other three. "Isn't he something?"

Sacker looked at the massive dog in amazement. "He is…something. But why is he here?"

"He guards the place when we are not around. Mr. Holmes acquired this property when the previous owner died. Boomer was just a pup when he bought the property. Burke and I trained him. He is great with the horses and keeps trespassers away."

"Wait…Sherlock Holmes owns this place?" Sacker asked, incredulously.

"Oh no. Sorry if I gave the wrong impression. Mycroft Holmes owns this property. The horses, the carriage, the dog, the whole lot, it all belongs to him. He also employs a groomsman to maintain the horses and to care for Boomer."

"Are we displacing the groomsman tonight to house our guest?" Quartermaine asked.

"Oh no. McTavish, that's the groomsman, has a cottage in Caroline Place. He lives there with his wife and two boys. He is normally here during the day. He only uses the groomsman's shack to stay over if we are going to bring the horses back late at night."

"Well, then let's not tarry another moment," Sacker said, walking toward Sleeves. "Let's get our guest situated until Holmes arrives."

Quartermaine was about to follow Sacker when Hobbs reached out his arm to stop him. "Mr. Sacker, you might want to wait a moment and watch. Doctor, if you would please join us." Watson stepped away from Sleeves and rejoined the other three men. Then Burke and Boomer began to work together. "Up," Burke commanded. Boomer immediately rose and stood by his side. "Heel," Burke said, walking toward Sleeves. Boomer followed, until he was right in front of Sleeves. "Alert," said Burke. Suddenly, Boomer bared his teeth, growling and gnashing, then gave one thunderous bark. "Settle," Burke said directly, and the huge dog immediately sat down next to him. Burke walked closer to Sleeves and when he was nearly nose-to-nose with the man, he looked him squarely in the eyes. "Do not give me reason to turn this dog loose on you. Now, follow me."

Sleeves hobbled along behind Burke and Boomer. The other four men followed close behind. As they walked along, Hobbs looked at Sacker. "Isn't he something?"

"Quite impressive," Sacker replied, as he walked along with his colleagues, still watching the huge dog closely. "Has he ever attacked anyone?"

Hobbs continued to walk alongside Sacker, looking straight ahead. "We don't talk about such things."

Burke opened the door to the groomsman's shack and instructed Sleeves to enter. He situated him on the cot and undid the handcuffs from behind Sleeves back. He allowed him to rub his wrists to get some circulation back. Then he had Sleeves extend his hands in front of him and placed the cuffs on his wrists. "Don't make me regret this." Then he turned to Boomer standing by the door. "Down, Boomer." The huge dog moved to a small rug in front of the parlor stove and laid down. Burke walked to the door. He looked to his colleagues. "Which of you is going to relieve me in two hours?"

"I will," Hobbs said. "I am not sure anyone else has quite worked up the desire to work with Boomer yet."

"Right then. I will see you in two hours." With that, he closed the door to the shack.

"What now?" Hobbs asked.

"We wait," Quartermaine replied. "When Holmes arrives, I am sure he will have a plan."

"I could eat something," Sacker interjected.

"What a surprise! Ormond Sacker is hungry...again."

Sacker just smiled. Watson then spoke up. "I may have just the thing," he said, walking over to where he had left the haversack. "I brought some things along, on the off-chance some of you may not have had the opportunity to have any dinner." He held out the haversack to display the contents. "You can thank Mrs. Hudson for the repast. She put the whole thing together and then thrust the bag into my hands as I was leaving Baker Street." The men gathered around the table and each man took a sandwich and a bottle of ale. They each found a place to sit to enjoy their much-appreciated refection. The carriage house was momentarily quiet.

Shortly before eleven, the entry door to the carriage house opened. Each man spun about, their pistols at the ready. Sherlock Holmes stepped inside, closed the door behind him, and looked to his colleagues. "You can lower your weapons, gentlemen. I am alone. But it is good to know you are all alert and primed."

Watson walked toward Holmes. "Where have you been, Holmes? I cannot believe you have been with Mycroft and the prime minister all this time."

"Believe it, Watson. There is much to tell, but I would prefer it not be at this precise moment. Where is our prisoner?"

"He is in the groomsman's shack. Burke and Boomer are guarding him," Hobbs answered.

"Why is Burke even in there? He could easily have just left Boomer on guard duty. I doubt our prisoner is foolish enough to try to outmaneuver a dog with lightning-fast reflexes that weighs nearly eight stone."

"We all wanted to be sure you had a prisoner to question when you arrived, so we weren't taking any chances," Sacker replied.

"Unless, of course, you take into account the chances taken by these two in getting him here," Watson interjected. "Do you have any idea how they brought him here?

Holmes quickly scanned the carriage house. "Since I see no corpse lying about, I presume Mr. Sleeves was delivered to us inside the coffin, which now sits empty. Is he alive, Watson?"

"By some accident of fate, yes, he is alive."

"And does he seem to have all of his faculties?"

"If you are asking me if the man is cogent, I would have to say he is."

"Then these two men have accomplished their task, however extraordinary their measures to deliver him here may seem." Holmes looked to Sacker and Quartermaine, "Gentlemen, well done."

"Mr. Holmes, do you want me to get the Black Maria ready to transport our prisoner?"

"I think not, Nathaniel. It might be best to question our prisoner here. The more disoriented he is, the more likely it is he will be willing to cooperate."

Sacker interjected, "I think he is pretty well disoriented, Holmes. He was unconscious for more than eight hours, and when Dr. Watson woke him, we told him he was being held in the south of France. I doubt he knows where he really is, or who, besides Quartermaine and myself, has him captive. We have been careful not to use names in front of him, so he only knows Algernon and I, from our confrontations with him in Paris. But, that said, I would not wager on his cooperation."

"We shall see. Will someone go and bring out our prisoner so we can begin our conversation?"

Watson, Sacker, and Quartermaine moved nary a muscle. They just turned their eyes to Hobbs, who laughed and said, "I'll go, Mister Holmes. These three gentlemen have not quite gotten comfortable with Boomer yet."

Holmes laughed aloud, then noted, "I am not surprised by the doctor's reaction. In the main, he does not have a fondness for dogs. And I will excuse Messrs. Sacker and Quartermaine for their reluctance. They have been through quite a lot in the past few days, and Boomer can be intimidating when first encountered. For myself, I cannot wait to see the big hound. Please fetch Mister Sleeves, if you will."

Hobbs went out the back entrance to the carriage house and was gone only a few minutes. When the door opened again, Boomer bounded in and headed straight away for Holmes, who dropped to one knee and extended his arms to greet the dog. He rubbed behind the dog's ears and gave him a big hug. "Good boy, Boomer. Settle," he said, and Boomer immediately sat at his side.

While Holmes was occupied with Boomer, Hobbs had retrieved Sleeves and led him out, with Burke trailing behind. Still restrained hands and feet, Sleeves hobbled forward toward Holmes, who turned to Watson. "Doctor, could you please get the stool for our guest?"

Watson retrieved the stool and set it down directly in front of Holmes. Sleeves shambled forward and sat.

"Could someone remove the restraints from this man? He looks uncomfortable." Burke took out his keys, undid the handcuffs and shackles, and then stepped back. "Do you need some water before we begin?" Holmes asked.

"Before we begin what? And who, in bloody hell, are you?"

"For the moment, I am your inquisitor. Names are not important." Holmes' tone suddenly became resolute. "What is important is that you understand clearly just how bad the situation is for you. You are in unfamiliar surroundings, with unforgiving people, who are the only beings on this good earth that know you are alive. The rest of the world believes you are two days deceased. So, no one is going to rescue you from this place.

Your best and only option is to cooperate fully with me. It is the only way you can improve your already dismal fate. Do we understand each other?"

Sleeves sat quietly for a moment, looking down at the floor. Then he raised his head, glared at Holmes, and spoke. "Here is what I understand. When I arrived, I was told I was being held in the south of France. If that is so, why do all of you speak the Queen's English? I have not heard one of you speak a word of French. You also tell me I have been declared dead, and no one knows I am here. But no one can show an ounce of proof that what you say is true. So, what I believe is that you have kidnapped me, and I am being held somewhere in Paris. You are hoping that I am stupid enough to believe your ruse. You threaten me with some unspoken fate in hopes that I will tell you what I know about the organization which employs me, pays me handsomely for my work, and has protected me from people like you. Well, I am nobody's fool. I will tell you nothing. Do what you will. When I am rescued from this place, wherever it is, you will all pay with your lives."

Holmes turned to his colleagues, "Well, what say you, gentlemen?"

Sacker spoke first. "That's the Sleeves I have come to know and despise. Arrogant to the last."

Quartermaine chimed in next, "If he is going to tell us nothing, I say we just turn Boomer loose on him. It will make the newspaper reports correct in all respects, save the date of his death, which will be off by a day or two."

"Yes, but then which of you wants to clean up the mess? When Boomer finished with him, there would be pieces of him all over the carriage house. Besides, all that screaming would disturb the horses. No, that just won't do." Holmes turned, looked at Burke, and then down at Boomer.

Burke took the cue and gave one command. "Boomer, heel." The dog immediately rose and moved to his side.

Holmes then walked over to the table and dragged the lone wooden chair back to where Sleeves sat on his stool. Holmes set the chair down and straddled it, facing Sleeves. "Actually, here is what is going to happen. Since you have been declared dead, you will have no trial. You will, instead, be taken, under a new name, to the French ship-of-the-line Intrepide, where you will be shackled below decks until you are delivered to Ile Royale in French Guiana, specifically Prison Saint-Laurent-du-Maroni. From there you will be transferred to Saint-Joseph Island, where you will spend the rest of your miserable life in solitary confinement, in silence and darkness. No one, outside of the men in this room, will know who you really are, or where you have been sent. No one is going to rescue you."

Sleeves face drained to a pallid white, "You...you...you have no authority to do such a thing."

"On the contrary," Holmes retorted, withdrawing a folded paper from his inside coat pocket. "I have written authority from the Prime Minister of France himself. You know, the man you hired assassins to kill? The ship is in port at Calais, and your passage has already been arranged." Holmes turned to Hobbs. "Would you please place the restraints back on Monsieur Homme Perdu?" Hobbs gathered up the shackles and handcuffs and placed them back on Sleeves, who sat, shaken and abased, his mind pouring over the desolate future Holmes had painted for him.

"Will you take our prisoner back to the shack until we are ready to deliver him to the ship?" Holmes said to Hobbs, who gathered up the defeated Sleeves and led him away. Burke quietly signaled for Boomer to follow, and the dog loped to Hobbs' side and then trotted obediently one step behind. When Sleeves was out of earshot, Watson looked at Holmes, somewhat stunned. "Holmes, were you serious about sending that man to Devil's Island? Is that what took you so long today? You actually got the Prime Minister of France to sign this man's death sentence?"

Holmes held up the paper he had shown Sleeves. "Oh, this? This is nothing. It contains my notes from my meeting with Mycroft and the PM. But, to answer your question directly, yes, I was serious about sending that man to Devil's Island. My only regret would be I could not send the rest of the organization he works for to that prison to keep him company. It would be a fitting end for all of them. For now, however, we will let him ponder his future for a time, then we will make another run at him."

"So, what took twelve hours to discuss with your brother and the PM?'

Holmes looked about. "Are there no more chairs in this place?"

"Why would there be a plethora of chairs in this *carriage house*, Holmes? It is, after all, a stable, and there is rarely a great call for chairs in a stable."

"Point taken, Watson. I was just hoping we could all sit together and discuss what transpired today at 10 Downing Street."

"There are bench seats on either wall inside the Black Maria," Burke remarked. "We could all sit in there."

"Rather unorthodox, to be sure. But nothing about this day has been conventional. Can you go get Mr. Hobbs, Jonah? All of you should hear this."

"What about Sleeves, Mr. Holmes?"

"Put Boomer at the door, Jonah. I think that dog should be enough deterrent for Mister Sleeves."

Burke returned with Hobbs and all six men climbed into the Black Maria and sat across from each other on the benches that lined the side walls. Holmes began, "It seems we have underestimated the scope and daring of the organization we have been trying, with little success, to identify. They have been one step ahead of us at every turn. But, on October twelfth, they perpetrated their most brazen attacks and, I believe, accomplished just what they intended."

"But, Mr. Holmes, we stopped the assassinations in Portsmouth and in Paris. They failed."

"You are correct, Hobbs. The assassination attempts failed. But, while we were focusing our attention on preventing the deaths of the heads of state in England and France, they accomplished their primary objective."

"Which was what exactly, Holmes?"

"Robbing the Bank of England and Banque de France, Watson. Those explosions reported in the newspapers were purposefully inaccurate and bereft of detail. Both governments were careful about what information was provided. If the public were to learn the extent of the thefts, there would be panic and mayhem. But, before I tell you any more I must have each of you swear not to repeat anything I am about to tell you."

"Is it really that bad?"

"It is. Now swear to me, all of you."

The five men all swore themselves to secrecy, then Holmes continued, "Between the two banks, the thieves made off with the equivalent of a quarter million pounds sterling."

"Good God, man," Watson exclaimed. "How is that even possible?"

"It appears the explosions were detonated after the thefts had been completed. When the fire brigades arrived at each site, they found the front doors of each bank locked. When they finally managed to pry open the doors, no one was found inside, and the fires were extinguished in short order.

When the police subsequently arrived, they found people bound and gagged at the rear of each building, relatively unharmed, and completely unawares as to what had transpired. The only person unaccounted for at each bank was the bank manager. These were carefully planned and exquisitely executed robberies."

"You sound as though you admire these thieves, Holmes."

"I appreciate the level of mathematical precision in the planning and execution, Watson," Holmes replied. "But I still view them as criminals and intend to bring them to justice." There was a long pause as Holmes' mind began whirling. Then, he spoke again, more excitedly than before, "And the precision in the planning and execution of this endeavor has offered a clue to the mastermind behind all of this mayhem," Holmes said, jumping up and clambering out of the Black Maria.

"How so, Holmes?" Watson asked, following him out of the carriage. With no response, he called out, "Holmes? Holmes!"

Walking away and waving a hand in the air, Holmes deferred, "Not now, Watson. I must think." Then he began pacing to-and-fro the length of the carriage house.

The other men climbed out of the Black Maria. Quartermaine approached Watson. "What is happening, Doctor?"

"As a physician, I would say Holmes is in a heightened state of cogitation, no longer aware of us or his surroundings. As his friend and colleague, who has seen this behavior before, I would say, if anyone has a deck of cards, we could best while away the time with a game of cribbage."

*   *   *   *   *

CHAPTER FOUR

Aboard the Cato

One hour crawled by, and Holmes remained deep in thought, Hobbs busied himself by brushing down Samson, one of their two Shire horses, and cleaning its hooves. Burke walked back to the groomsman's shack to look in on Sleeves. Sacker and Quartermaine took advantage of the quiet, climbed back into the Black Maria, and stretched out on the benches to try and catch forty winks. Watson dragged the solitary chair from where Holmes had left it over to the table, reached into his haversack, and took out his notebook. He sat down and began to pen his recollections of recent exploits with Holmes, thinking there may be another story fit to print in the *Strand* magazine. The carriage house was eerily quiet. Another hour passed. Suddenly, Holmes stopped pacing, threw his hands up, and shouted, "That's it!"

Watson looked up with a start, stood up and rushed toward Holmes. "Good heavens, Holmes, are you all right?"

Holmes clasped Watson by the arms and looked him straight in the face. "There is not a moment to lose, Watson. We have to stop the money from changing hands."

"What are you talking about?"

"The stolen money…from the banks…we have to intercept it before it gets to its intended destination. Where is everyone? Halloo?"

Hobbs stepped out of one of the horse stalls where he had been working. Burke came bursting through the back door of the carriage house and ran toward Holmes. Sacker and Quartermaine stepped down from the Black Maria. "Holmes, what is all the noise about?" Sacker said, dazedly.

As everyone drew near, Holmes explained, "Everything that has been done, all the false documents, the assassination attempts, everything…has been designed as a series of distractions. The end game for this organization was always the money. And I believe if they get their hands on it, their reign of terror has only just begun. So, gentlemen, we must stop that money from reaching its destination."

"But how exactly do we do that, Holmes?" Quartermaine asked.

"We catch the thieves who committed the robberies."

"Simple as that?" Sacker retorted cynically.

"Nothing this complex is simple, Ormond. But, whatever we do, it must be done quickly. I do not believe the money will be held in any one place for long. However, it will take some time for the money taken in Paris to make its way to England, and the money here in London will need to be hidden until the thieves feel it is safe to move it."

"What makes you think all the money is coming to England?"

"Logical deduction. I have concluded that, whoever the mastermind of this organization is, he is an Englishman. He surrounds himself with Englishmen as his seconds, Colonel Sebastian Moran and George Harrington Sleeves, to name only two. The money will come here."

"So, do you have a plan, Sherlock?" Sacker asked.

"I do, but it will require participation of everyone here."

"We would expect nothing less. What would you have us do?"

"Since you asked, Algernon, I will start with your part. In the morning, as soon as the telegraph office opens, I need you to reach out to Henri Loze and ask for his assistance, which may prove difficult, because I am aware he has been in meetings with Messieurs Floquet and Goron regarding the very matter I need you to pursue with him. We need to scoop up every capable thief in Paris who may have had any knowledge of this robbery."

"If I may, Mister Holmes, there may be a quicker way to get the information we need. When Sacker and I were in his office yesterday, Henri already appeared to be under duress from Floquet and Goron regarding this matter. He mentioned his meeting with them and was clearly distracted by whatever orders he had been given. Besides, I think Sacker and I know others in Paris more suited to the task."

"Then I will leave it to your discretion, Algernon. However, I have need of Ormond for another assignment."

"Whatever you need, old man. I am at your service."

"I would not be so quick to volunteer, my friend. You haven't heard the job yet."

"Whatever it is, Holmes, I am your man."

"As you wish, Ormond. I need you to get Sleeves to talk. Specifically, I need two pieces of information from him. First, I need to know if he employed anyone at Banque de France to assist in the robbery. Second, and more importantly, who his contact is within the criminal organization about which he is so fond of bragging. And time is of the essence."

"By any means necessary?"

"Yes. By any means necessary."

"Holmes!" Watson exclaimed.

Holmes held up his hand. "Watson, you and I do not have time to get into moral arguments at the moment. You will just have to trust that Ormond would not do anything that I would not do."

"That is exactly my worry."

"Holmes, can Burke and Hobbs assist me?"

"What do you have in mind?"

"A boat ride."

Holmes thought for a moment, then a smile crept across his face. "Brilliant!" he said, then turning to Hobbs and Burke. "Gentlemen, will you please assist Mr. Sacker with anything he may need?"

The two men walked over to Sacker, and then the three of them moved away to discuss what Sacker had devised. Watson turned to Holmes. "What does that leave for us to do?"

"First thing in the morning, I need you to go to the Bank of England and ask for Alfred de Rothschild. Tell him I sent you. I need you to ask him, in confidence, if he is aware of anyone who might have been involved in the robbery."

"What are you going to do while I am at the bank?"

"I am going to be working with Shinwell Johnson to find out which thieves in London were hired to accomplish the robbery."

"Don't you think Scotland Yard is already on that task?"

"I am sure of it, Watson. But we do not have the luxury of time to wait for their plodding efforts to bear fruit, if ever that may happen. I am equally sure Shinwell and I can unearth the information I need in a day or less. And once we know who was involved, it should take little time at all to find out where and to whom the money was delivered. Did you hear that, Mr. Quartermaine?"

"I did, Mr. Holmes. It was my thought exactly. Find the thieves, then find the money."

"You would make a fine detective, Mr. Quartermaine."

"Thank you, sir," Quartermaine said, glancing over at Sacker. He smiled and Sacker gave a slight nod, then continued his conversation with Hobbs and Burke. "Mr. Holmes, if you have a moment, I would like to speak to you about that very thing."

"Of course, Algernon. What is on your mind?"

The two men walked away from the rest and their conversation was hushed and brief. Holmes patted Quartermaine on the shoulder. "If you think that best, I trust your judgment," he said quietly.

Within an hour, the carriage house grew quiet. Hobbs, with Boomer at his side, had moved to the groomsman's shack to guard Sleeves. Burke had gathered up three horse blankets and he, Sacker, and Quartermaine had returned to the back of the Black Maria to get what sleep they might. Holmes and Watson returned to Baker Street. The night would be short, and the forthcoming morning would test each man's abilities.

When the groomsman, Angus McTavish, arrived shortly after daybreak, he was surprised to see the buzz of activity in the carriage house. Hobbs had already harnessed Samson and Hercules, the two black Shire horses. Burke was inside the wagon, covering the barred windows with cloth. When McTavish walked around to the back of the wagon to view what Burke was about, he was greeted by the ever-energetic Boomer, as the dog leapt out of the wagon and bounded in circles until the groomsman finally calmed him by stroking his head and giving him a piece of sourdough bread from his pocket. When Hobbs saw McTavish, he walked over to the old man and was about to explain the reason for their being at the carriage house. McTavish stopped him. "No need to explain, Mr. Hobbs. I have worked for Mr. Mycroft Holmes long enough to know his peculiar and particular ways are not the ways of other men, and it is best not to ask or even wonder what he and his brother, and those who work for them, might be up to. So, do what you need to do. I'll not be in your way." Hobbs thanked McTavish for his understanding and then asked him for a favor. The groomsman smiled and nodded. "I know just the place." He crossed to the table, scribbled an address on a scrap of paper and brought it back to Hobbs. "Give me an hour and everything will be waiting for you when you arrive." McTavish tipped his cap and was on his way.

Sacker came through the back door and strode up to the other two. "Are we ready to go?"

"Whenever you are," Burke replied. "Is our prisoner ready to go?"

"He is. Are you sure we will be able to hire a launch on such short notice?"

Hobbs smiled. "No worries. It is taken care of, Mr. Sacker. As soon as you get Sleeves aboard, we can be on our way. Or, do we need to wait for Mr. Quartermaine?"

"No need to wait on Mr. Quartermaine. He left before dawn. He has other fish to fry. I will go fetch Sleeves and then we can be off." Sacker walked toward the back of the carriage house, and quickly returned with Sleeves in tow, shackled about the ankles, handcuffed with his hands behind his back, and a black hood pulled over his head. He led him to the Black Maria and helped him up into the wagon. He attached another pair of handcuffs to the iron ring on the wagon wall and then hooked Sleeves' handcuffs, so he was securely attached to the sidewall of the wagon. "Wouldn't want you to fall and break something before we get you to the launch that will take you to the frigate bound for French Guiana and your final prison cell," Sacker said, stepping to the back of the wagon and closing the doors. He pounded on the roof of the Black Maria, then sat down, as the wagon pulled out of the carriage house, halting outside only momentarily so Burke could close the carriage house doors. Then they were off.

Hobbs and Burke sat atop the Black Maria and felt the chilled mid-October wind on their faces, as the two black steeds trotted on, along the road that took the wagon past Poplar, then Canning Town, and on to Barking. Hobbs was careful to drive along open country roads, avoiding passage through the towns. The thirteen miles to their destination would take more than three and a half hours, but it would give Sacker time to try to coax information from Sleeves. For his part, Sacker never showed signs of frustration or anger when Sleeves remained quiet and unyielding after each query he posed. After nearly three hours, Sacker stood up and pounded on the roof of the carriage. "How much longer?"

"Less than an hour to the launch," Hobbs called back.

Sacker sat down again and leaned in toward the hooded Sleeves. "Hear that, Sleeves? In less than an hour you will no longer be my problem. We'll take you on a launch to the French frigate, you will be given a number, shackled to a plank in the bowels of the ship, and never heard from again."

74

To assure Sleeves would not hear their conversation, Burke asked Hobbs in hushed tones, "I thought you said we were getting a launch from Gravesend-Tilbury Ferry. Tilbury is still, at best speed, at least two hours more from here."

"The launch is coming from Gravesend-Tilbury, but the pilot is sailing the launch to meet us at Dagenham Docks. McTavish gave me the directions this morning and said he would take care of the arrangements. The launch should be waiting for us when we arrive."

The remainder of the trip to Dagenham Docks was uneventful. Hobbs and Burke chatted, as friends will do, about things unrelated to the task at hand. It was, in fact, the first time in a fortnight that they had any time at all to divert their focus from anything other than what Mycroft Holmes had assigned them to do. The convivial conversation took the sting out of the crisp autumnal wind that braced them as they rode along. Sacker, on the other hand, while protected from the elements, grew more exasperated with each passing minute. Despite his best efforts, Sleeves had not spoken a single word since he had been shackled inside the wagon. The one hope that danced around in Sacker's brain was that, once they got Sleeves onto the launch and the reality of his incarceration on Devil's Island seemed imminent, he might break and finally make a clean breast of things. But the longer Sleeves refused to say anything, the less hopeful Sacker was of that outcome.

It was nearly half past ten when the Black Maria pulled through the Dagenham Docks' main gates. Burke hopped down and pulled a stevedore aside and asked where hired launches might dock. The stevedore pointed to a shack about three hundred yards along. Burke thanked the man and climbed back atop the carriage. As they approached, a stout, burly-looking fellow came up a ramp that led up to the shack. He waved. Hobbs pulled on the reins and the carriage came to a stop. Burke hopped down again and walked away from the carriage with the man until they were out of earshot. They had a short conversation and Burke returned. He pounded on the carriage door. "We are here."

When Burke opened the back doors, Sacker climbed out. "What should we do with our prisoner?" Speaking loud enough for Sleeves to hear, Sacker replied, "Leave him chained up in the dark. He needs to get accustomed to what the rest of his life will be." Burke slammed the door shut, leaving Sleeves shackled to the carriage sidewall. Then he and Sacker walked over to speak with the pilot.

The pilot extended his hand. "Thaddeus Etheridge, at your service." Pointing at the launch, he continued, "That there is the Cato, she was retired from service in 1883 from the Gravesend-Tilbury Ferry service. She hain't much to look on, but sturdy as the day she was built, she is. And fast enough, too, if'n we have need of it."

"Fast should not be a concern, Mr. Etheridge. As long as she stays afloat, we will be satisfied," Sacker replied.

Thaddeus Etheridge looked at Burke, "Angus didn't tell me you'd have landlubbers aboard on this trip." Then he turned to Sacker again. "The Cato is forty year old, but still seaworthy. And, lest you forget, I am doing this as a favor to Angus McTavish and came without question. You might think to do the same."

"My apologies, Mr. Etheridge. It was not my intention to disparage you nor your launch. But I do have one question. Is there any chance you speak French?"

"Angus didn't say anything about speaking French when he telegraphed this morning, But, to answer your question, mate, I was in the Merchant Marine for twenty year. I speak some French and a bit of German. Why do you ask?"

"The prisoner we are going to bring onto your launch has been given the impression he is somewhere in the south of France and is being brought to a French frigate off the coast of Calais to be shipped to Devil's Island. He will not be able to see you, but it would be helpful to maintain the ruse if he heard a French voice on the launch."

"Anything else Angus forgot to mention?"

Burke stepped forward. "We have no specific destination, Thaddeus. We are hoping that the boat ride itself will cause the prisoner to break down and give us the information he has been reluctant to give up thus far."

"So, this is a pleasure cruise then?"

Sacker became impatient. "Sir, there is nothing pleasurable about what we are trying to accomplish. The man we are trying to break is responsible for the deaths of many people, and other capital crimes too numerous to mention. So, if you will do your part, we will do ours. And, no matter how this turns out, you will have the thanks of all of us here, the Crown, and Mr. Sherlock Holmes."

"Mr. Sherlock Holmes! Why didn't you say that in the first place? Mr. Holmes saved my brother from the hangman's noose a few years back. There isn't anything I wouldn't do for that good man. Get your prisoner and let's cast off. I will take you wherever you want to go."

Sacker headed back to the Black Maria with Burke and Hobbs. Hobbs said he would find a place for them to house the carriage and the horses until they returned while they collected Sleeves. Burke opened the doors at the back of the carriage. Sacker climbed in, unshackled Sleeves, and led him to the back of the carriage. Then, without warning, Sleeves threw himself to the floor of the carriage, rolling over on his back so as to prevent Sacker from catching his arms again. When Burke tried to grab his legs, Sleeves kicked wildly. When they finally got hold of Sleeves again and got him to his feet on solid ground, his head dropped to his chest and a faint whimper could be heard from beneath the hood. "Please, don't do this."

Sacker and Burke walked on either side of Sleeves, sometimes leading, sometimes dragging the shambling Sleeves to the top of the ramp that led down to the launch. Thaddeus Etheridge and Hobbs were waiting when they arrived. Burke spoke to the pilot, "Bonjour, monsieur, etes-vous le pilote du lancement de la prison Cato?"

Thaddeus replied, "Oui, monsieur, je suis le pilote. Qui transportons-nous?

Burke answered, "Un prisonnier se dirige vers Ile du Diable."

To which Thaddeus replied, "Compris, emmeme-le a bord." Then he led the men down the ramp to the Cato.

Sacker led the still hooded and shackled Sleeves to a length of bench along the starboard side of the launch. He sat him down and then sat next to him. As Sleeves sat whimpering pitiably, Sacker leaned over close to him and whispered, "Soon I will be rid of you, George Harrington Sleeves, and none too soon to suit me. You didn't want to talk to any of us in loyalty to an organization that can do nothing to save you from your fate. So, I say goodbye and good riddance!"

While Hobbs stayed up at the helm with Thaddeus, Burke came back to sit across from Sacker. He winked and said loudly, "We are about twenty minutes away from the French frigate Resolue, then we can be rid of this brigand once and for all. Although, I honestly do not know why we are going to all this trouble. If it were up to me, I'd say we just toss him overboard and let him drown."

"No, I want this criminal to waste away in absolute solitude with nothing but his thoughts haunting him. It is a more fitting retribution for his deeds than a swift dispatch by guillotine."

Hearing the two men revel in his demise, Sleeves jumped up, turned, and tried to throw himself overboard into the water. Sacker reached out and caught hold of the handcuffs behind Sleeves' back and jerked him backward. Sleeves fell to the deck of the launch. "What did you think you were doing, Sleeves? Did you actually think we would let you end your life so easily? I have been trying to bring you to justice since Germany, and while you will not be tried in a court of law, your sentence of life in solitary confinement will suffice for me." Sacker and Burke picked up Sleeves by the arms and sat him back down. "How much longer to the frigate?" Ten more minutes was the reply. "See there, Sleeves, just ten more minutes. See what your silence and loyalty has purchased for you?"

Sleeves was finally a beaten man. He slumped on the plank bench and began sobbing uncontrollably. His emotions took hold of him, he dropped to his knees on the deck and, after a time, grew silent. Then he murmured an inaudible utterance. Sacker looked at Burke, who just shrugged. Neither man had understood whatever Sleeves had said. Then it came again, slightly louder, yet still unintelligible. Sacker bent down next to Sleeves. "Did you say something?"

Sleeves, almost in a whisper, answered, "Don't do this. I will answer your questions."

Sacker looked at Burke in amazement. "Did you hear him?"

"I did. He said he would talk."

Sacker leaned in closely to Sleeves. "You have a bit more than five minutes before we turn you over to the French. I will not turn this launch around until you tell me something to convince me to do so. So, listen carefully. Who is the mastermind of the organization you work for?"

"I do not know."

"Full speed ahead!"

"Wait! Wait! I cannot tell you what I do not know. I never met or talked to whoever runs the organization. I only ever spoke to one man, who always spoke for the man in charge, and who kept the identity of that man a great secret. It was dangerous to even inquire about him."

"Then who did you report to?"

"Colonel Sebastian Moran. As far as I know, he is the only man who knows who the real mastermind of the organization is."

"That is all you know? I think maybe the French will be able to get more out of you, once you have been locked away and beaten for a year or two. I see the frigate Resolue. Stay the course."

"Wait! Please? There is one more thing."

"Speak, man. We are almost at the frigate."

Sleeves knelt shaking on the deck of the launch. He paused for a moment, weighing his words, realizing the next words he spoke would determine his fate. He began again, timorously, "Only once did I ever hear Moran even refer to someone who had given him his orders. He was about to shoot a man for disloyalty. He held the gun to the man's head and, as he

79

pulled the trigger, he said 'compliments of the professor.' When he realized I was standing there, he glared at me and pointed his pistol at my chest. At that moment, I thought he was going to kill me too, for overhearing what he had said. I do not know why he did not shoot." There was a long pause, then, "That is all I know, I swear it."

"Turn the boat around. Back to port, if you please, sir."

Sacker and Burke stood Sleeves up and sat him back on the plank bench on the starboard side. "Well, Sleeves, you saved yourself a trip to Devil's Island, for the moment. However, if anything you have told us proves untrue, you will be back in chains and on your way to French Guiana so quickly it will make your head swim."

When the Cato arrived back at Dagenham Dock, Sacker led Sleeves up the ramp, as Burke and Hobbs went to retrieve the Black Maria. Once they had Sleeves securely shackled inside the wagon and closed the doors, Sacker strode back to Thaddeus Etheridge. "I am obliged, Mr. Etheridge. Your launch is a fine seaworthy vessel, and you played your part impeccably. Can I at least compensate you for your fuel?"

"Thank you, but no. I am still in debt to Mr. Holmes for what he did for my family. Besides, it is good to give Cato some exercise now and again. It does the old girl and me good to be on the water. Be on your way. You have a good long trip back to London. And give my regards to Mr. Holmes when you next see him." The two men shook hands, and Sacker walked back to the carriage. Burke locked him in with Sleeves, then climbed up next to Hobbs, and they were back on the road to London.

*   *   *   *   *

CHAPTER FIVE

An Ignominious End

That same morning, Sherlock Holmes was up and about as London embraced another grey dawn in the midst of autumn. Watson came out of his bedroom, somewhat bleary-eyed, and walked gingerly over to the teapot on the dining table and poured himself a cup of Earl Grey. Holmes smiled at his colleague. "Glad to see you are finally awake, Watson."

Watson looked disdainfully at Holmes. "How could anyone sleep with you banging about in here, Holmes? What has you so wound up this morning?"

"I was out this morning to Shinwell's shanty, but he was not there. When Wiggins arrives, I will have him gather the Irregulars and find Shinwell for me. But, as yet, I have not seen the boy," he said, glancing at his pocket watch.

"Could be that it is not yet seven in the morning. I know this will come as a shock to you, Holmes, but the rest of the world does not abide by your impracticable hours. The boy is usually here at eight on the dot. And, when he arrives, he will be gone again and about your bidding within five minutes of his arrival. And I know I am wasting my breath, but you need to adopt some modicum of patience."

"How can you ask such a thing of me, Watson, when every minute counts if we are going to catch the thieves who perpetrated this theft?"

Giving up, Watson took his coat from the coat-tree and strode to the top of the stairs. "I am going to get a morning paper. By the time I return, I hope either Wiggins has arrived, or you have decided to harness your energy for later in the day, when you will be in need of it." Watson walked down the stairs and out onto Baker Street in search of a news-boy.

Shortly after Watson returned with his paper, at precisely eight o'clock, Wiggins came bounding up the stairs. "Mornin' Mr. 'olmes, wot 'ave you got for me today, sir?" Watson looked up from his newspaper, opened his pocket watch, and held it up for Holmes to see. He shook his head and returned to his paper.

"I need for you to round up the Irregulars and find Shinwell Johnson for me. When you find him, have him come here at once. And don't bother going to his shanty. I have already been there, and he was not at home."

"Course not, Mr. 'olmes. Most nights Shinwell is visitin' wif Miss Mabel 'argreeves. That is probably where oy'll find 'im."

Holmes looked mortified. "But...but...Miss Mabel Hargreeves is a single young woman. It would be inappropriate for Shinwell to be spending nights with her. You must be mistaken."

Watson dropped his newspaper into his lap. Wiggins just smiled. "Mister 'olmes, Shinwell don't spend the night wif Miss 'argreeves. 'e visits wif 'er and then, instead of comin' back to 'is shanty, 'e stays in the groundskeeper's cottage on 'er property. It's all proper and respectable. Shinwell finks the world of Miss 'argreeves."

"Well, if you think he is there, there is no need to gather up the Irregulars. Go to Shinwell and tell him to come here at once," Holmes replied, tossing a half-sovereign to Wiggins. "Tell him it is urgent."

"Since you have business to conduct with Shinwell, Holmes, I am going to attend to *my* appointed task. I will see you when I return from the bank. Taking his hat and overcoat from the coat rack, he proceeded down the stairs and out onto Baker Street, where he caught a cab and instructed the driver to take him to Threadneedle Street. When the hansom arrived in front of the Bank of England, Watson climbed out, paid the driver, and made his way up the stairs. He was somewhat surprised as he entered the bank lobby that there was business per usual. There was the unmistakable redolent pong that lingers anywhere a fire has recently burned, yet there did not seem to be any visible signs of a sizeable fire or an explosion in the lobby proper. Clerks dashed about caring for the needs of their customers. All seemed proper and normal. Watson proceeded up the stairs to the first floor where the executive offices lined both sides of that level. He strode up to the secretary's desk, situated in the center of the hallway. He identified himself and asked to speak to Mister Alfred de Rothschild on urgent business, on behalf of Sherlock Holmes. The slender, smartly besuited, young man behind the desk detachedly asked Watson if he had an appointment. Watson said he did not, reiterating that his business with Mister de Rothschild was both personal and extremely urgent. Seemingly unimpressed, the young man informed Watson that Mister de Rothschild was currently in conversation with some gentlemen from Scotland Yard and, no matter the urgency of his business, he would have to wait. Watson glared scornfully at the young secretary, turned, walked to a finely polished oaken bench along the wall, and sat down.

Nearly half an hour passed and finally the door to Mister de Rothschild's office opened. Inspectors G. Lestrade and Athelney Jones stepped through the opened door. Lestrade thanked an unseen individual for his time and the two men turned to leave and were surprised to see Dr. Watson seated outside the office. "So nice to see you, Doctor, without that pompous arse Holmes," Athelney Jones remarked smarmily, continuing to walk toward the stairs. Watson stood up to respond, but Lestrade stepped alongside and uttered under his breath, "Speaking of pompous arses."

Watson turned to see a smiling Lestrade facing him. "Why do you tolerate such a vituperous Neanderthal on the force?"

"I have no authority nor latitude to question who I am partnered with from case to case. I do as I am told, Doctor. Such is my lot. I tolerate Jones the same as I would a cankerous tooth. I deal with it in silence until I can arrange to have it excised." Then Lestrade smiled and winked at Watson, drawing a small flask from his inside coat pocket. "And occasionally a sip of good scotch whisky." Then both men laughed. "I must catch up with Jones before he does something I will need to undo. Good to see you, Doctor. Sincerely." Lestrade nodded to Watson and strode toward the stairs.

The young secretary called to Watson. "Director Rothschild will see you now, Doctor," he said perfunctorily, walking over to open the office door.

Watson entered the office and Alfred de Rothschild strode toward him, extending a hand in greeting. "Dr. Watson, please come in and sit down. I hope you did not have to wait too long. I had to speak with Scotland Yard about the unfortunate incident that occurred here two days ago. But I am at your disposal now. How can I be of service?"

"Well, sir, I come on behalf of my colleague, Sherlock Holmes. And, to be direct, I have come to speak to you, in strictest confidence, about that very same unfortunate incident. I hope you do not mind. Holmes would have come himself, but he is otherwise occupied."

"I do not know how much more there is to say on the matter. As I explained to the gentlemen from Scotland Yard, there was an inexplicable explosion and a small fire, which was extinguished by the fire brigade when they arrived. As I am sure you could see from the business being conducted downstairs, we are carrying on as if nothing happened."

Watson thought for a moment on how precisely to proceed, musing about what Holmes would do in such a circumstance. Then he confronted Rothschild. "Sir, I do not mean to be indelicate, but I have knowledge of what actually occurred in this bank the other afternoon, and I would prefer if you would be so kind as to be forthright with me. As I said at the start, I am here on behalf of my colleague, Sherlock Holmes, so whatever you would say to him, you can say to me. Before you begin again, however, let me state what I know the facts to be. There was an explosion, which triggered a fire. Prior to those events, however, the front doors to the bank had been barricaded, everyone in the bank at the time was taken to a place of safety at the rear of the building, bound securely, and gagged. The brigands who perpetrated these deeds were not here for murder, they were here to commit a robbery. Said robbery was executed with precision and a great sum of money was removed from this bank. I am unaware of the exact sum, but I know it to be substantial. Have I left anything out?"

"Your description was unimpeachable, Doctor. I take it your information was gleaned from a discussion with Mr. Holmes, who was informed, I am sure, by the prime minister himself."

"You are correct, sir. And if we are to succeed in capturing these criminals, there are details which only you can provide. The first thing I need to ask is, have you completed an accounting of how much was taken?"

"I do not know to the penny, but to the best of my knowledge, the criminals made off with approximately one hundred eighty thousand pounds in notes and gold."

Watson was taken aback for a moment by the sheer enormity of the theft. Then he proceeded. "Sir, Holmes believes the thieves may have been assisted by someone from inside the bank. Is there anyone in your employ whom you would consider a suspect in that regard?"

"There is only one manager who has not been accounted for since the robbery. His name is Archibald Hanover. He went missing straightaway after the robbery. He hasn't reported to work since then. We sent a runner to his home to check on him, but his wife said she had not seen him since he went to work that day. She was in a frightful state."

"Did you mention any of this to Scotland Yard?'

"I must admit, I was more than a trifle vague with Scotland Yard. In truth, I did not trust one of those men. He struck me as pompous, arrogant, and an incompetent blowhard. So, I told them as little as I could. I told them I was having the Pinkerton Agency look into the situation and would let Scotland Yard know if their assistance was required. In truth, I was also afraid whatever I told them might be leaked to the press. Fifteen years ago, I nearly lost my employment with this institution because of an article in the London Times regarding an elaborate forgery scheme that was perpetrated against this bank by four American sharpers and, to my chagrin, to which I was a hapless victim. If it were ever found out that, once again, the Bank of England fell prey to criminals on my watch, my employment as director of this institution would come to a swift and infelicitous end. Only a few people within this institution know the actual scope of the loss. While I have contacted a friend at Pinkerton's to look into this matter, I am hoping your colleague can provide a swift resolution to this unfortunate event."

"It is our hope as well, sir."

"Is there anything else you need, Doctor?"

"You have been most helpful, sir. May I call on you again if we need anything further?"

"Without a doubt." Rothschild shook hands with Watson and escorted him to the door. "Please thank Mr. Holmes for me, if you will."

Watson nodded and exited the office. He walked down the stairs, through the lobby, and out onto Threadneedle Street, where he flagged cab and instructed the driver to take him to Baker Street. By the time he returned, Holmes had already left with Shinwell Johnson. He hung up his overcoat, took up his newspaper, reclined in his chair, and sat reading his paper in the uncustomarily quiet apartment.

*   *   *   *   *

When Shinwell Johnson arrived at Baker Street with Wiggins, Holmes quickly apprised him of the situation and the need for alacrity in the discovery of the criminals responsible for the bank robbery. Once Shinwell understood the task in front of them, he was quick to suggest the inclusion of Jack Dawkins. "There isn't anyone knows the underbelly of this 'ere town like Dodger. And free of us lookin' for these blighters will get the job done right quick…if it can be done at all. You know it h'aint likely they're gonna 'ang on to that much money for long. We need to track 'em down straightaway, gov'nor, or they'll be in the wind."

"If you think it best to bring Dodger along, let's go find him."

"Tell me where we can meet in an hour and oy'll find Dodger. You need to change your clothes, Mr. 'olmes. The places we'll be goin' you can't be dressed like a Bond Street dandy."

"Understood. Meet me in Regent's Park, on the main walkway to Jenkins Nursery, no later than eleven this morning. We can proceed from there." Heading toward his bedroom, he waved at Shinwell as the big man left.

Shortly before eleven, Shinwell Johnson and Jack Dawkins entered Regent's Park from Chester Terrace and strolled along the walkway toward

86

Jenkins Nursery, all the while keeping a close eye out for Sherlock Holmes. As they walked along, Dawkins tapped Shinwell on the arm. "Oy fink that's 'im, Porky," he said, pointing at the same grizzled old man he had seen once before outside the Boot Tavern some weeks previous.

"That's 'im, awlroit," replied Shinwell, striding toward the old man. "Ay, ya ol' geezer, wot you up to this mornin'?"

The old man looked at the two men, "Lookin' for a little plunder this mornin' oy am. So, shall we be about it?"

Shinwell looked about to make sure there were no inquisitive ears nearby, then lowered his voice. "Mr. 'olmes, I told Dodger wot it was you'd be lookin' for but it seems word's already on the street about the robbery."

Dodger added, "But most are too skitterish to talk. Seems someone involved got 'is froat slit and tossed in the Thames. Put the fear o' God in the rest. But oy do know one filcher wot might be willin' to chirp about it if 'e's paid well enough."

"Then let's start with him."

"We'll 'ave to hire a carriage, then. Can't walk to where 'e's at. This bloke is stayin' in a row 'ouse in Lambeth."

Holmes turned immediately and looked for a carriage. The three men had to walk a good way before a driver was finally flagged down. Holmes had to pay the driver in advance before he would let   three such questionable characters into his carriage. As they climbed in, Dodger called up to the driver, "Roupell Street, Lambeth, if you please, driver."

After nearly an hour, the driver called down, "We're in Lambeth. Any particular address you lookin' for on Roupell Street?"

Dodger poked his head out of the carriage window. "Anywhere 'long 'ere will do noicely."

The carriage came to a halt and the three men climbed out. They walked along Roupell Street until they came to Number 26. "This is it. You two best stay 'ere whiles oy go inside. Free of us might make 'im a bit jumpy, if ya know what oy mean. Oy'll be back as soon as oy explain to 'im why we're all 'ere." Dodger knocked on the door, as the other two stepped back out of sight.

"Who is it?" a timorous voice asked from behind the door.

"Jocko, it's me, Dodger. Open up. Oy 'ave a business proposition for ya."

The sound of a heavy latch sliding back could be heard and then the door opened no more than a crack. Jocko Connelly peered from inside. Dodger stepped to where he could be seen. "Wot business are ya talkin' 'bout?"

"Me and my friends want to talk to you 'bout the Bank of England job. Oy know you weren't in on it, but maybe you know who was. My friend 'ere is willin' to pay right 'ansome for wot ya know. An' you 'ave the word of Jack Dawkins no one ever will know who told us wot. Can we come inside? I fink talkin' in private will be better for all of us, pryin' eyes an' all out 'ere, if ya know what oy mean."

The door opened wider, and the three men entered quickly. Once inside, Jocko Connelly slammed the latch closed again and crossed nervously to a wooden chair across the room, a limp on his left side clearly noticeable. He was a small man, and frail. He had a round face, with a shock of black hair. He had a small, barely noticeable scar above his right eye, which looked as if it had been with him most of his life. His eyes were dark, almost black, amplified by the dark circles beneath them. His clothes were threadbare, and his shoes were worn. The furnishings in his house were not much better. A woman, looking older than her years, dressed in a faded blue muslin dress, encircled with a once-white apron, entered from the kitchen. Without a word, she looked at Jocko. He looked back at her and shook his head. "You don't need to be 'ere, Myrtle." She turned and scurried out of the room. A moment later, the men heard the back door close. "We're alone now. Wot can oy do for ya?"

Holmes spoke up. "If there is anything you can tell us about the men who robbed the Bank of England a few days ago, there's ten guineas in it for you."

Jocko looked queerly at Holmes, then at Jack Dawkins. "Who is this bloke, Dodger? 'e don't sound like no street tough ta me."

"Ya don't need names do ya, Jocko? All ya need ta know is 'e's my friend. An' if oy say 'e'll give ya ten guineas for wot ya know, that should be enough. An' oy say 'e will."

"Awlroit, awlroit. But wot's Shinwell Johnson doin' 'ere wif ya?"

"Just came along to make sure nuffing 'appens to us. Never know where we might 'ave to go to get wot we need. Wif Shinwell along, h'aint too many blokes goin' to brace us, if ya know wot oy mean."

"Can we get down to business, please? Time is not on our side, Dodger," Holmes reminded him.

"Righto, guv'nor. Awlright, Jocko. Wot can ya tell us?"

"Can oy see the ten guineas first?"

Holmes withdrew ten gold coins from his pocket and thumped them down on the small wooden table in the center of the room. "They are yours to keep, Jocko, if you have anything to tell us."

Jocko rose from his chair and hobbled over to the table. He reached for the coins. Holmes quickly covered them with his right hand. "Information first, coins after." Jocko returned to his chair, stared at the floor for a few moments. Then he looked up at Holmes. "About a fortnight ago, a slippery lookin' bloke came around askin' where 'e might find a grafter who could provide toughs who 'ad turned a trick or two of strong-arm work and a peter man who could open a box on the quiet. Oy 'eard 'e tried to draft some toughs from the Fitzroy Place Gang in Regent's Park, but they weren't 'avin' none of it. Then oy know 'e went to the New Cut Gang 'ere in Lambeth and they wanted no part of wot 'e was pitchin' eivver."

"Oh, oy know them boys. They h'aint got the stomach for bank robbery, nor murder neiver."

Jocko continued. "Oy 'eard 'e finally spoke to Mary Carr from the Forty Elephants, an' she agreed to set 'im up with some of 'er girls to gambol about inside the bank while the uvvers were doin' the deed. An' she arranged a meeting with George Whitehead from the High Rip Gang. Far as oy know, they provided the muscle 'e needed. Those boys are the ones you need to be lookin' out for, and they are a vicious bunch." Jocko shifted his focus from Holmes to the gold coins on the table. "Do oy get my pay now?"
Holmes turned to Shinwell and Dodger. "Do we need anything else from Jocko?"

Dodger replied. "Oy know the gangs 'e's talkin' about. An' if they are still in London, oy know where to find 'em. Not that oy would want to find 'em, mind ya, just the free of us. Takin' our lives in our 'ands we'd be, if ya know what oy mean."

Holmes looked back at Jocko. "Thank you, Jocko. Take the money. And take my advice. You and Myrtle find a place to disappear for a while. This whole matter should be settled in a week. If your information proves to be true, and you would be willing, I could use a man like you from time-to-time to listen to what goes on in this part of the city and pass it on to me. Of course, I would pay you for your time."

Jocko looked curiously at Holmes. Shinwell leaned over the small man. "'e takes good care of blokes like us, Jocko. You should fink on 'is offer."

Then Holmes turned to Dodger. "Take a look outside and see if we can leave unnoticed. I don't want to raise any suspicions about our being here, or put Jocko or his woman in danger."

As Dodger peered out through the window, Jocko moved to the table as quickly as his game leg would take him and snatched up the coins. Then he tugged on the coat sleeve of Holmes. "There's a back door leads to an alleyway. You could go out that way an' won't no one be the wiser." The three men passed through the small kitchen to the back door and were gone. As they walked away, they heard the sound of a heavy latch slamming shut.

"That went well, don't ya fink, Mr. 'olmes?"

"We shall see, Dodger, we shall see. What do you think of Jocko's story?"

"Wot? Do you fink Jocko was lyin'?"

"I do not. I just find it curious that he knows as much as he does."

"I don't understand, Mr. 'olmes," Shinwell began. "If you believe 'is story, why are you surprised at what 'e knows?"

"I misspoke. I just find it curious he knows as much as he does, and he is still alive to tell us."

"You don't know the 'affovit, Mr. 'olmes," Dodger replied. "Jocko is riskin' a lot talkin' to us.

That gammy leg of 'is was no accident. 'e used to be in the New Cut Gang, and 'e was one of the best snakesmen in all of London. Then one night the gang got into it wif the Monkey Parade Gang in Whitechapel, and one ov'em blighters sliced 'is leg up pretty bad. That finished 'im. Now 'e lives on what 'e can earn as a day laborer shovelin' coal and wotevver 'is Myrtle can earn workin' as a 'ousemaid. That money you gave 'im will help a lot, Mr. 'olmes."

Momentarily nonplussed, Holmes cleared his throat, then quietly uttered, "It was not charity, Dodger. He earned that money, fair and true."

"It was still a good fing ya did, Mr. 'olmes."

"Nevertheless, we need to get back to Baker Street at once. There are plans to be made, if we are going to retrieve the stolen money before it changes hands." Holmes picked up the pace, and the three men hurried along the alleyway, eventually coming out onto Brad Street. Holmes flagged a carriage. As the three men climbed in, he called up, "221B Baker Street, driver." And they were off.

As dusk approached, the three men arrived at Baker Street, and climbed the stairs to Holmes' lodgings. When Holmes reached the top of the stairs, he found Watson, sitting in his favorite chair, one finger pressed to his lips. Watson pointed across the room to the dining table, where Burke and Hobbs were seated quietly. Next to Hobbs sat George Harrington Sleeves, shackled hands and feet, with a dark hood over his head. Holmes turned to Shinwell and Dodger and signaled for them to say nothing as they entered. The three men crossed the room. Holmes went to his bedroom and removed his disguise. He returned moments later, wiping the remnants of adhesive from his face with a damp cloth. He looked about at the gathering of people in his lodgings, his mind racing. Then he walked quickly to his desk. He scribbled something in his notebook. He tore out the page and walked to the dining table, handing the paper to Burke, who read the note and then turned to Sleeves.

"Sleeves, when is Mary Carr delivering the money from the Bank of England job? And to whom is she delivering it?"

Sleeves sat up with a start. "How do you know about…" Then he stopped abruptly and shook his head. "Don't know what you're talking about," came the muffled reply from beneath the hood.

Hobbs leaned over to Sleeves, grabbed his arm, and whispered venomously, "We are not so far from the water that we can't take you back, you pigeon-livered ratbag. So, you'd be wise to answer this man's questions."

A flurry of curses came from beneath the hood. Then Sleeves was quiet again for a moment. He began quietly. "I was responsible for the collection of money in Paris, which is scheduled for tomorrow night. However, I will not be there, thanks to being snatched up by you scrubs and declared dead." Sleeves' voice grew stronger. "The money taken from the Bank of England job was to end up with Colonel Moran. But I'm sure he will have someone else do the collecting. The only things he's good at are giving orders and killing people."

"Where and what time is the exchange in London to take place?"

Sleeves became agitated. A muffled scream came from beneath the hood. "I told you, I am not responsible for the London exchange. I know it is to be tomorrow night, but I do not know when exactly."

"Where, Sleeves?"

Sleeves did not answer. Hobbs grabbed him by the arm. "I've had enough of you, Sleeves. Get up. We're going back to the boat. The French can deal with you." Sleeves thrashed about, trying to wrench himself from Hobbs's grip. Burke rose from his chair and grabbed Sleeves' other arm. The two men started to drag him toward the doorway. A pitiful moaning came from beneath the hood. Then, "Regent's Park!" he screeched, collapsing to the floor. Then quietly he muttered, "They're to meet at Regent's Park."

Burke knelt down next to the broken Sleeves. "When and where were you to make the exchange in Paris, Sleeves?"

Utterly defeated, Sleeves gave up the information meekly and quietly. "Midnight tomorrow night. A two carriage exchange, each one coming from opposites sides of the Champs de Mars. The carriages would stop, the money would be transferred, and the carriages would disappear into the night. I would then deliver the money to Colonel Moran two days hence in London."

Burke looked up at Holmes. "What should we do with him now?"

"Take him back to the carriage house. We will deliver him to the authorities in the morning."

"I'll go get the wagon," Hobbs said, helping Burke stand Sleeves back on his feet and placing him in his chair. "I'll be right back."

As Hobbs left to fetch the Black Maria, Holmes looked to Burke. "What has become of Ormond? Was he not with you all day today?"

"That he was. On the way to Baker Street, he asked us to stop by his apartment in Grosvenor Square. He said he wanted a change of clothes. We dropped him there two hours ago. I expect he will arrive here in short order." Burke took hold of Sleeves and led him to the top of the stairs.

"I hope so. We have much yet to do. Take care that Mr. Sleeves is well-sequestered. He has much to answer for in the morning." Hearing the rumble of the Black Maria outside, Holmes looked out the window of his apartment. "Your carriage has arrived, Mr. Sleeves. Fare thee well."

Burke led Sleeves carefully down the stairs. He opened the door at the bottom of the landing. He glanced up and down Baker Street, checking for any unwanted lookers-on. Hobbs hopped down from the seat atop the wagon. He went around to the back and opened the doors, as Burke led the still shackled and hooded Sleeves around to the back of the Black Maria. As Burke held onto Sleeves' arm to help him up into the wagon, one shot rang out. Sleeves' head snapped back, and he fell back dead on the cobblestones. Instinctively, Hobbs and Burke ducked behind the wagon, drew their revolvers, and looked about furtively, trying to ascertain the location of the shooter. Burke turned and looked up at the second-floor window to Holmes' apartment. The light suddenly went out. Then the sound of footsteps could be heard coming down the stairs. A slender silhouette appeared for a split-second in the doorway, then the person made a dash for the wagon. It was Holmes.

"Mr. Holmes," Burke whispered. "There's a sniper. He shot Sleeves. I think he's dead."

"He was on the rooftop across the street. I saw the muzzle-flash from my window. When I turned down the light, I saw the shadow of a large man across on the rooftop. He was moving away, toward the back of the building. I believe he has fled."

"If we move quickly, we can catch him as he descends."

"Nathaniel, do not pursue him," Holmes replied, reaching to catch Hobbs by the arm. "He has a long gun, and the darkness is his advantage. Moreover, if the shooter is whom I suspect, you would more likely be prey than hunter. Besides, we need to tend to Sleeves. If he is not mortally wounded, we need to get him to hospital as quickly as we can. If he is gone, we need to remove him from the street before we gather onlookers."

The three men moved cautiously. Holmes and Burke went to the fallen body of Sleeves. Hobbs kept a watchful eye on the rooftop across the street. As Holmes and Burke carried Sleeve's body to cover behind the Black Maria, Watson came running from the doorway. "Give me some room to examine him." He knelt down beside the fallen Sleeves and pulled the blood-soaked hood from about his head. As soon as he removed the hood, the magnitude of the damage to Sleeves' skull was evident. The bullet had entered just above his left ear and had exited on the right side, shattering his jaw. In his military service, Watson had seen such wounds before and knew the consequences. "There is nothing anyone can do for this man. The only saving grace for this wretched soul is that he never knew what hit him. He was dead instantly."

"Help me lift him into the wagon, gentlemen," Holmes requested of Burke and Hobbs.

"I'll go up and get something to cover the body," Watson said, with rancor in his voice. When he returned, he had a worn muslin sheet, which he carefully draped over the body. When he finished that grim task, he turned to Holmes, with a saturnine expression. "Holmes, you must find these men and stop them. These senseless murders must come to an end."

*   *   *   *   *

CHAPTER SIX

Best Laid Plans

As the men did their part on the street below, Watson, having nothing more to say, turned and walked back to the doorway to 221B. He went up the stairs to the darkened apartment, walked over to his favorite chair, and sat. Holmes came up the stairs behind him, walked to the window, and pulled the curtains closed. He turned up the lamp again and turned to his colleague, who sat motionless in his chair. "Watson, whatever it is that has you in such a state needs to be put aside for the present. I need your assistance. More to the point, I need you to be in full possession of your faculties."

"I have never been more in possession of my faculties, Holmes. It is you, it seems, who does not have a full grasp of the gravity of the situation in which we find ourselves."

"What are you saying, Watson?"

"I am aware of two murders today alone. While you were out today, Lestrade came by. He had seen me at the bank this morning and assumed we were involved in some sort of an investigation on their behalf. He told me they had found the body of the bank manager who had gone missing. They pulled his body out of the Thames this afternoon. His throat had been slit. Lestrade said it was the coroner's conclusion that he had been in the water for two days. That means these villains killed that man right after the robbery. Now Sleeves. You have got to stop these men, Holmes."

"I intend to do just that, Watson. But, I cannot emphasize strongly enough there is much to do and precious little time to accomplish it all. I need your help more than ever I have. When the authorities arrive, will you please accompany the body of Sleeves to the coroner? I need you to make sure whomever they assign to examine his body does not make a mess of things. I have sent Burke to Scotland Yard to fetch Inspectors Lestrade and Gregson." Holmes paused to make sure Watson was listening, then he continued, "We need to report the killing of Mr. Sleeves, but we need to explain why he was in our custody in the first place. Of those inspectors at the Yard, I find few to be competent detectives, and I trust fewer still. But I believe Lestrade and Gregson have a sense of uprightness and duty, and can be trusted to provide the assistance necessary over the next twenty-four hours. Can I rely on you to do that?"

"Need you ever ask, Holmes?" Watson replied, rising from his armchair and moving to the coat tree to retrieve his hat and overcoat.

Then Holmes turned about and realized Shinwell and Dodger were still there. "Sorry, gentlemen, I was completely caught up in the moment and forgot you were here. I have no further need of you tonight. However, I would appreciate it greatly if you could be here first thing tomorrow morning. I believe I will have work for you then."

"No worries, Mr. 'olmes, dead bodies tend to give me the quivers anyways. See you in the mornin'." Shinwell rose from his chair and headed for the stairs, with Jack Dawkins close behind. Without another word, the two men descended the stairs, stepped out onto Baker Street, and disappeared into the chill and dank of the London night.

While Burke was off to Scotland Yard, Hobbs had busied himself by fetching a bucket of water to splash Sleeves' blood from the cobblestone. He had also done his best to wipe down the inside of the wagon and was closing up the back doors when a hansom cab pulled up. Ormond Sacker climbed out, paid the driver, and then walked back toward the wagon to speak with Hobbs. When Hobbs saw Sacker, he wiped his hands best he could, and strode toward his colleague.

"Why is the wagon here, Nathaniel? And where's Sleeves? Is he upstairs with Holmes?"

Hobbs turned and walked toward the back of the wagon. "No, he's in here." Hobbs opened the doors again and stepped back. Sacker stepped around to the back of the Black Maria and saw the covered body lying inside. "Sleeves?"

"Shot in the head. He was dead before he hit the street. Rooftop sniper. One round. Never saw him. Though Mr. Holmes seems to think he knows who fired the shot."

"Is Holmes upstairs?"

"He is. Best get up there. He's been waiting on you."

"What about you?"

"I am waiting for Burke to return with Scotland Yard. Then Dr. Watson and I are going to take Sleeves to the coroner. Holmes is going to try to explain what we have been doing for the past few days. I am fairly certain he could use reinforcements for that."

"You clearly don't know Holmes as well I do. The man could natter his way out of well-nigh any situation. And Scotland Yard is certainly no match for the indomitable Sherlock Holmes. But I will lend whatever assistance I am able. Take care that Sleeves is the last man killed tonight, Hobbs. Neither Sherlock nor Mycroft would be pleased if Watson or you were to come to a bad end. It would grieve me as well." Then he strode to the door at 221B, entered, and bounded up the stairs. Before Sacker could say a word, Holmes barked, "Dash it all, Ormond, where have you been?"

"I smelled like a fish-monger after dragging Sleeves up and down the Thames, Holmes. I went to my flat to wash off the stench of the river and change my clothes. I am here now. What do you need of me?"

Watson looked across at the two men. "I will be on my way, gentlemen. Unless there is anything more you need of me, Holmes." Holmes did not reply. "Then I am certain you two can function without me for the present." Then Watson headed down to join Hobbs on the street.

Holmes watched his colleague depart and then refocused his attention to Sacker. "We have less than twenty-four hours to formulate a plan to retrieve the stolen bank money. A gang of criminals will be delivering it tomorrow night in Regent's Park."

"And what, precisely, Holmes, do you want me to do with that information?"

Holmes continued. "The brigands we will encounter tomorrow evening will not surrender easily. It seems there were two gangs involved in the robbery of the Bank of England. They are members of the Forty Elephants and the High Rip Gang, two of the most dangerous gangs in all of England. So, we will need to be prepared to deal with them appropriately."

"Holmes, are you suggesting a gun battle?"

"I am hoping it does not come to that, Ormond. But we must be prepared for the worst."

Sacker sat down at the dining table. "Sherlock, old chum, this sounds incredibly dangerous. I would suggest we enlist Scotland Yard for this enterprise. Because, as things stand, it is you and I and Watson. Oh yes, and Burke and Hobbs, if they are willing." He paused for a moment, then mused, "I wish Quartermaine were joining us. That is the man you want at your side in a gun battle. He is deadly accurate."

"Well, if I were to guess, by now he is reunited with his comrades in Paris, searching for the criminals who robbed Banque de France. He left before dawn. He told me he was going to catch the first train to Dover. Since it has been nearly eighteen hours since he departed, I suspect he is by now on the case. Which reminds me, we need to get a telegram to him first thing in the morning. Before Sleeves was silenced, he provided information on how and where the money is going to change hands in Paris."

"Well, Holmes, he is most likely staying at the same hotel we stayed before, Le Grand Hotel du Louvre. You could send a telegram to his attention there. But, if you want to guarantee your message will be received, I would suggest you also send a telegram to him to the attention of Prefect Henri Loze at the Prefecture of Police in Paris. That should ensure he gets your message, one way or the other."

"I will send Billy to the telegraph office first thing in the morning, and I will send telegrams to both addresses, as you suggest. I must make Algernon aware of the transfer of the stolen money planned for tomorrow midnight. If Quartermaine is as smart as I believe him to be, he and his colleagues can lay a trap for those criminals and, if all goes well, all the stolen money will be retaken by the end of day tomorrow."

"Right, Holmes, what could possibly go wrong?"

Sacker's words never registered with Holmes, his mind already spinning through innumerable solutions to the problems that lay ahead. He strode over to the mantel and picked up his churchwarden clay pipe. He plunged it into the old Persian slipper and filled the pipe to the top with black shag tobacco. He used a tong to pick up a bit of burning coal from the fireplace to light the pipe, walked to his desk, and sat. A ribbon of smoke rose from the pipe as Holmes mused on the options coursing through his brain. In the next moment, Holmes opened the lap drawer on his desk, withdrew two pieces of packet note paper, then put pen to paper. In short order, he had drafted both telegram missives to be delivered to the telegraph office in the morning. He set those aside and sat back again, never speaking a word to his colleague, who sat quietly and patiently, knowing all-too-well the nature of the man sitting across the room. Finally, there was a knock at the door at the bottom of the stairs. After a brief conversation between Mrs. Hudson and the late-night visitors, the sound of two men climbing the stairs could be heard. Without looking up, Holmes said quietly, "Ormond, could you please let Inspectors Lestrade and Gregson in?"

"Certainly, Holmes, I wasn't doing anything anyway." Sacker walked to the door and greeted the two Scotland Yard detectives. "Gentlemen, please come in and have a seat. We have much to discuss."

Holmes rose from his desk and walked over to the dining table, bringing his desk chair with him. Once he and Sacker were seated, he began. "Let me introduce you to an old friend of mine. He will be joining us for this conversation. Gentlemen, this is Ormond Sacker." Sacker nodded to the two Scotland Yard men. "Ormond, that is Inspector Lestrade and that is Inspector Gregson," he said, indicating each man, respectively. "Now that we have the pleasantries out of the way, I need to have your word that what is about to be discussed in this room tonight will go no further. You cannot even report what I am about to tell you to your superiors."

Lestrade immediately balked at the idea. "Holmes, do you realize what you are asking of us?"

"I do indeed, Lestrade. But if what I am about to tell you were to ever become public knowledge, the very stability of the Empire could suffer irreparable damage. I need your word you will hold what you are told in confidence."

"And if we do not?" Gregson asked.

"Then this meeting is over, and you have my apologies for calling you out at such an hour." When there was no response, Holmes began to rise from his chair. "Very well, then. Goodnight, gentlemen. Watson, please see these men out."

"Hold on, Holmes. You are asking a lot of us."

"You do not know the half of it, Lestrade. But you know me. I would not ask this of you were it not absolutely necessary. Now do I have your word?"

"You have my word, Holmes."

"Gregson?" queried Holmes.

Gregson looked over at Lestrade, who nodded. Then he looked back at Holmes. "I give you my word, Mr. Holmes."

For the next hour, Holmes detailed the events of the past month, explaining how the governments of three European countries had been threatened, how the leaders of those countries had been protected from assassination attempts, and how a criminal mastermind had orchestrated every step of every mission from an unknown sanctuary in complete anonymity. Then he added, "While we have been able to capture or dispatch many of the perpetrators of these crimes, we have yet to identify the mastermind behind it all. Over time, we have gotten closer to learning his identity and, in fact, had someone in custody who may have been able to lead us ever closer. Unfortunately, he was killed earlier this evening in front of this lodging. That is part of the reason you have been called."

"Holmes, I have known about some of what you have told us tonight. In fact, I helped you capture some of those brigands. And I have not said a word to anyone, as you requested of me before. But the murder of one more criminal, despite the fact it happened at your doorstep, does not raise itself to the level of secrecy you are requesting of us. I do not understand."

"If you will let me finish, Lestrade, I think you will understand. There is more to this story, but since we have paused on the dead man at my doorstep, let us deal with him first. When you arrived, I presume you noticed the Black Maria stopped in front of this residence. Well, Dr. Watson is waiting for you, with the body of the dead man. He will accompany you, if you can rouse a coroner tonight, to examine the body."

"Why the urgency about this dead man, Mister Holmes?"

"If I may, Sherlock?" Sacker interjected. Holmes nodded. "The reason for the urgency regarding this particular man is because he was declared dead three days ago in Paris by the Prefect of Police. His name is, or was, George Harrington Sleeves, and he was one of the men who ran things, first in Berlin and then in Paris, for whomever this mastermind is, to whom Holmes has referred. He was caught in Paris and brought here under, shall we say, *unusual circumstances,* to try and learn the identity of that mysterious man. No one should have known he was here. But someone knew. And that someone killed him before he could tell us what we wanted to know. So, I think it safe to say we are being watched...all the time. That is part of the reason for secrecy."

"The other part deals with what I have to tell you now. Lestrade, Watson tells me you were at the Bank of England on Threadneedle Street this morning with Inspector Jones."

"That is correct, Holmes."

"I also understand that the director, Alfred de Rothschild, did not provide much information to you about the incident a few days ago."

"That is also correct. Which seemed damned peculiar to me, to be honest, Holmes."

"No doubt, Lestrade. But there was a reason why the director did not divulge much information to you. And now we come to the part to which I have required your word. In addition to the explosion and fire at the bank the other day, there was a robbery of significant proportion."

"How significant?' Gregson asked.

"One hundred and eighty thousand pounds sterling, to their best estimate."

"Good God, Holmes!"

"Precisely, Lestrade. A monumental sum, which if made known to the public would, most assuredly, cause a panic and a run on the bank, but, more disastrously, could undermine faith in the government."

"But there is more, Inspector," Sacker added, looking again to Holmes, who nodded. "At the same time the robbery was occurring here in London, the Banque de France was robbed. We believe it can be safely assumed it was orchestrated by the same criminal organization. The thieves in Paris made away with roughly one million francs. You should know that robbery has also been kept from public knowledge. With the precarious nature of the political environment in France, the French President is very concerned with the French populace learning of it. So that information, too, must be held in strictest confidence."

"So, gentlemen, the real reason you were asked here tonight is to ask for your assistance in recovering the stolen money from the Bank of England robbery."

Gregson interjected, "No offense, Mr. Holmes. But that is clearly a job for Scotland Yard."

"None taken, Inspector. And, if Scotland Yard had an inordinate amount of time to solve this case, and inexhaustible resources, I have no doubt, at some point, you might solve it. Meanwhile, the Bank of England would have to make public their security had been breached and their funds depleted. Faith in both the Bank of England and, likely, the government of Queen Victoria would be damaged beyond repair. Never mind what would happen in France. More to the point, Inspector, the most nefarious and dangerous criminal gang ever to set foot here or on the Continent will have enriched their coffers to the tune of over three hundred thousand pounds. Enough to finance that criminal enterprise ad infinitum. But here is the rub. I have specific knowledge that all the stolen money, both here and in Paris, is going to change hands in the next twenty-four hours. And I know roughly when and where in London the exchange will take place. So, do I have your cooperation or do I not?"

There was a long pause. Then Lestrade spoke. "What do you need of the two of us, Holmes?"

"I need you here at six o'clock tomorrow night. We shall leave from here to intercept the criminals. And, if it is any consolation, Inspector Gregson, when this is all over, and the money has been retaken, you and Inspector Lestrade can return the money to the Bank of England. Of course, no one but you and they will ever know what has transpired, but you will be forever in their good graces. I need no such attribution."

"We will be here, Mr. Holmes," Lestrade said assuredly.

"Good. Now, if you and Inspector Gregson could go with Dr. Watson to the coroner. You will also find Mycroft's men, Messrs. Burke and Hobbs waiting there with him. They can drive you to the morgue, and when you have concluded your business there, they will take you back to Scotland Yard, or home, if you prefer."

"We can find our own way home, thank you all the same, Mr. Holmes," Gregson replied, donning his coat and hat.

"As you wish, Inspector. Thank you for your assistance, and goodnight."

The two Scotland Yard men departed. Holmes walked to the window to watch the wagon drive away. Impulsively, Holmes looked across to the rooftop across the street once more. Then he looked down again to the street to make sure the Black Maria was not being followed. When Holmes turned away from the window, Sacker looked to Holmes. "What exactly do you want me to do, Holmes?"

"Can you be here first thing in the morning, Ormond? Before Scotland Yard returns tomorrow evening, we need to find out precisely what time and precisely where in Regent's Park the exchange is going to take place. I will have two of my colleagues here in the morning. We can split up and cover more ground. I believe, with two teams on the street, we will be able to learn what we need to know. And, Ormond, we will be dealing with the hoi-polloi of the London streets, so please dress accordingly."

"I will do my best to look as tatty as I can. And, if it does not meet with your approval, I am sure I could always find something from your closet that will do the job. I will be here promptly at seven in the morning. Is there any chance Mrs. Hudson could have breakfast for us? I am usually ravenous at that hour."

"I do not usually have breakfast, Ormond. A cup of Earl Grey and I am ready for the day. But I am sure Mrs. Hudson can fix something for you. I will see you in the morning." Sacker watched as Holmes dragged his chair back to his desk, sat down, picked up his pipe again, took a stick match from a small tin on his desk, struck it, and lit his pipe. Sacker stood for a moment, expecting some final comment from his friend. Realizing Holmes had returned to the cloistered chamber inside his head, he took his hat and coat and left.

*   *   *   *   *

The next morning at Baker Street, Sacker arrived, as promised, promptly at seven o'clock. Within fifteen minutes of his arrival, a beaming Mrs. Hudson delivered a tray flaunting a full English breakfast, comprised of two eggs, cooked just enough so the yolks remained runny, two Wall's sausages, cooked tomato slices, an ample helping of baked beans, fried mushrooms, and two slices of sourdough toast. She set out the repast on the dining table, then filled a teacup with piping hot Earl Grey tea. She smiled sweetly at Sacker, then apologetically said, "Sorry, Mr. Sacker, but I dinnae have any bacon for ye. Had I known sooner you'd be wanting breakfast this mornin', I would've sent Billy to market yesterday."

Sacker took Mrs. Hudson by the hand and smiled. "Mrs. Hudson, this is a braw and bonnie meal, fit for a king. It needs nothing more. I thank you and my stomach thanks you."

Mrs. Hudson looked over at Sherlock, as he strode out from his bedroom. "It is nice to know there are some men who appreciate a woman's work in this house." Then she started for the stairs.

"Ah, Missus Hudson, you are esteemed in my heart above all other women in this house."

"I am the *only woman* in this house, Mr. Holmes, and, lest you forget, I'm also your one and only landlord."

"A fact I never forget, Mr. Hudson, and one for which I am most appreciative. No one else would tolerate such a man as myself. You are an exceptionally uncommon and unusually brilliant woman, ma'am."

Mrs. Hudson threw up her hands. "Wheesht! I'll not stand here and have you pull my leg. I am a busy woman and have things to do." Then she disappeared down the stairs. As she reached the bottom of the stairs, the front door opened, and Billy stepped through. She shooed the boy upstairs. "Best get up there, laddie. Mr. Holmes has a task for you."

Billy sped up the stairs and crossed the room to Holmes. "Morning, Mr. Holmes. Mrs. Hudson said you have a task for me."

"I do indeed, my boy," Holmes replied, taking two silver crowns from his vest pocket and handing them to Billy. He then turned and retrieved two envelopes from his desk, handing them to the boy. "Take these to the telegraph office and, this is important, Billy, tell the telegraphist these need to go out first thing this morning. Tell him you will wait for acknowledgement of receipt. When you get receipts for both telegrams, come back here and give the receipts to Wiggins. I will be out and about today, but he will find me. I am relying on you, my boy."

"I will not let you down, sir. Is there anything else?"

"That is enough, young man. Off with you now."

As Billy flew down the stairs, he nearly crashed into Watson coming up the stairs. When Watson entered the apartment, he strode over to the coatrack and hung up his overcoat and hat. "You need to put a bell on that boy, Holmes. That is the third time in recent memory that lad has nearly taken me down the stairs with him."

Holmes and Sacker both laughed. "How is it that you cannot hear that boy thundering down the stairs, Watson?"

Watson scowled at the two men. "I often have things on my mind when I am coming to see you, Holmes. The last thing I am anticipating is to be bowled over by some imp tearing down the stairs at breakneck speed. And, I must tell you, it is damned unnerving at this time of the morning."

Holmes and Sacker burst into laughter again. "I will say something to the boy, Watson, I promise. On a more serious note, have you any information regarding the recently departed Mister Sleeves?"

"That is why I am here, Holmes. I went to the morgue with Lestrade and Gregson last night. We were in luck since Inspector Lestrade was able to engage Dr. George Bagster Phillips to conduct the autopsy. I find him to be a skilled and capable surgeon. After conducting the autopsy, he concluded, as had I, that Sleeves was killed by a high caliber round entering on the left side of his skull and exiting through the lower right jaw. The damage to the man's brain was devastating. There was one curious thing, though. There were no bullet fragments found. Typically, when a bullet hits bone, shards from the bullet will be found in the adjacent tissue. During my field service to the Crown in India, it was not uncommon for this to be the case. In fact, in thinking back, I cannot remember a time when it was not so. No such fragments were found in this man's head. Holmes, I could only conclude that the velocity of the bullet was such that it passed through his head so quickly, it left no offcuts behind. I must admit, I have never seen anything like it in my practice as a physician."

"Did Phillips have any other conclusions regarding Sleeves' demise?"

"He did not. I did ask him to hold the body at the morgue under a John Doe for the time being. I promised to get back to him within two days regarding the disposition of the body. He agreed, only after Lestrade pulled him aside and explained that this was a matter of national security."

Holmes seemed alarmed at this mention. "Did he say anything more than that, Watson?"

"He did not have to, Holmes. Dr. Phillips immediately understood the gravity of Lestrade's words and the manner in which they were delivered. He did not ask any questions. He simply agreed to do as he had been asked. From the morgue, Lestrade and Gregson took their leave, and I caught a cab to my home. I believe Burke and Hobbs took the Black Maria back to the carriage house. When we parted company, they told me they were going to meet you here tonight at six o'clock."

"That is correct. Would it be possible for you to join us here at that time as well? I suspect tonight we will be having a meeting with the people who are now in possession of the money taken from the Bank of England. I would imagine you would want to be party to that meeting."

"Without a doubt, Holmes. Without a doubt. I presume you want me to bring my pistol with me?"

Then, there was a commotion at the bottom of the stairs, followed by the sound of two men coming up to the apartment. Shinwell Johnson and Jack Dawkins entered, followed closely by young Wiggins.

"It is good to see you, gentlemen. And, Wiggins, your addition to our assemblage could not have been more providential."

"Oy fought ya might need me today, Mr. 'olmes. So when oy saw Shinwell and Dodger 'eaded this way, oy tagged along. Wot can ya use me for, Mr. 'olmes?"

"Actually, Wiggins, I need you to stay here and wait for Billy to arrive. He will have some receipts from the telegraph office that I will need you to bring to me. I will be with the Dodger and we will likely be somewhere in Whitechapel. If you need to use some of the Irregulars to find me, gather the boys up and find us. It is important I know these telegrams have been delivered."

"Consider it done, Mr. 'olmes," Wiggins said, walking over to plop into Doctor Watson's chair. As he stepped close to the chair, he heard Watson clear his throat. Wiggins turned and gave a sheepish grin to the doctor, then he bent over and gave the seat cushion a few quick swipes with his hand. "Just clearin' the dust off for ya, Doctor. Oy know not ta sit there."

Holmes stifled a laugh. "You can sit in my chair, Wiggins," he said, pointing to the large high back chair across the room. Then he turned to Watson. "Watson, I will expect to see you this evening at six." To the rest of the men, he said, "Gentlemen, we have our work cut out for us and but a few hours in the day to accomplish our task. Our goal is to find out where the stolen Bank of England money will change hands tonight, when the exchange will occur, and who will be delivering it. Any questions?"

Shinwell spoke up. "Mr. 'olmes, since the Forty H'elephants was involved, do ya fink we'll be needin' a woman to 'elp us? Mind ya, oy'm not keen on havin' Mabel facin' any danger, but if ya fought it would be useful, oy could bring 'er along wif Mr. Sacker and myself. She could chat up the women we come upon."

"Thank you, Shinwell, but no. I don't think we need to put Mabel in harm's way. And, in point of fact, I am not completely convinced the Forty Elephants were anything more than a diversion during the robbery. I believe we will be looking for members from the High Rip Gang. And, I must admit, that fact has been bothering me since Jocko Connelly told us about it."

"What has you bothered, Holmes?"

"Ormond, I can understand why the Forty Elephants might be employed for this job. If you want to create a distraction, what is more distracting to most men than a bevy of attractive young women sauntering about in front of them? But why, when there are countless criminal gangs in London, would someone bring a gang from more than one hundred eighty miles away to rob the Bank of England in London? The High Rip Gang is not a London gang. Their territory is up in Liverpool."

"Think for a moment, Holmes. If this criminal organization wanted to be sure the London Metropolitan Police and Scotland Yard would not recognize these men at first sight, the best way to assure that would be to bring in outsiders. It is not at all unlike when I was in Paris. Sleeves recruited murderers from all over France to commit those assassinations. It must have taken him a good deal of time to recruit them, I'm sure. And, if these bank robberies were the end game of this organization, it is hard for me to believe they would not commit the same level of effort and spend the time necessary to recruit criminals who would do their bidding without question."

"You have a valid point, Ormond."

Then Shinwell spoke up. "Mr. 'olmes, when oy was in Parkhurst, there was a lot of blokes in there for committin' murders, and uvvers wot got put in there for fings like blowin' up stores and warehouses, and uvvers for settin' fires and uvver mischief. Lots of 'em blokes were from the gangs. Some of 'em were toughs, and some were just plain evil. But the worst oy ever came across were two blokes from the 'igh Rippers. They once gut a bloke for not givin' up 'is bread and water. If the need for this bank job was for some men who would do anyfing necessary, includin' murder, then oy'm not surprised they went and recruited them 'igh Rip blokes."

Holmes thought for a moment, then began. "Gentlemen, without a doubt, this is a most dangerous enterprise. And I will not ask any of you to risk your lives accompanying me in this endeavor. For myself, I have no choice in the matter. If I were to give up now, I might as well become a cloistered monk, for my life's work will be of no account. I will have allowed the most dangerous criminal organization I have ever encountered to succeed in establishing itself here and on the Continent. Therefore, I must proceed." He turned and started to head for the stairs when Sacker spoke up. "Well, my friend, I must say, that was a damned impressive speech. A tad melodramatic, to be sure, but damned impressive, nonetheless. Now that you have gotten that off your chest, what do you want the rest of us to do?"

Holmes, momentarily taken aback by Sacker's blunt assessment, stood motionless. Then he regained his composure. "With the four of us asking around, I think we will learn what it is we need to know in due course. And if there is any trouble, we will handle it directly. Dodger and I will start in Whitechapel. Ormond, if you will go with Shinwell, you and he could start in Piccadilly.   Let us meet at one o'clock at the Seven Stars Pub in Holborn to review our progress. Agreed?"

With no objections to the contrary, the four men went their separate ways. Holmes flagged a cab to take them to the outskirts of Whitechapel. Sacker waved down a cab, and he and Shinwell climbed in. Sacker directed the driver to take them to Piccadilly Circus. As the cab carrying Ormond and Shinwell made the turn from Baker Street onto Oxford Street, Shinwell inquired of his companion. "Mr. Sacker, would ya mind tellin' me wot the plan is when we get ta Piccadilly."

"Shinwell, first of all, I would prefer it if you would call me Ormond. We are working together, and Mr. Sacker sounds a bit too formal."

"Awlroit, Mister…er…Ormond."

"Now to answer your query, when we get to Shaftsbury and Regent Streets, I thought our best chance of spotting any of the Forty Elephant girls would be to walk back along Regent Street. Some of the finest shops in all of London are there, between Piccadilly and Oxford Streets. And from what I've read in the newspapers, this seems to be their favorite hunting ground. You could take one side of the street and I will take the other. If either of us spots any of the girls, we signal the other and, when we get to a quiet place, we can question her."

"Ormond, where do ya fink you'll find a quiet place along Regent Street? It's busy as a beehive."

"Point taken. Well then, if we find one of these girls, we will flag down a carriage and take her to Hyde Park and question her there. How does that sound?"

"Just one fing, Ormond. Ta the best of my knowin,' these girls work in pairs. So, we may need to be takin' a couple of 'em for a ride."

"Let us cross that bridge when we come to it, Shinwell, shall we?"

"Ormond, oy don't understand, h'aint no bridges between 'ere and 'yde Park."

111

"Never mind, Shinwell. No time to explain." Noticing that the cab was approaching Shaftsbury Avenue, Sacker called out, "Driver, stop here."

The two men climbed out and, as the cab pulled away, Sacker looked at Shinwell and pointed back toward Oxford Street. "You take the east side of Regent and I will take the west side. Wave if you see anything suspicious."

"Ormond, do ya even know wot you'll be lookin' for?"

"Why do you ask, Shinwell?"

"Oy've spent most of my life as a criminal. Oy know how to spy these filchers. Fact is, oy probably know some of 'em. No offense, but when you are on Regent Street, you're probably here ta buy somefing fancy for yourself, and the only pretty girls you see are buyin' fings too. Oy doubt you would know one of the Forty Elephant girls if she came up and picked your pocket."

"So, what are you suggesting, Shinwell?"

"Why don't the two of us walk down one side and then back up the uvver side. If oy spot one of these girls, oy will let ya know. Then we can take 'er to 'yde Park like you suggested."

"As you suggest, Shinwell. Let us begin."

The two men walked along Regent Street, keeping a watchful eye. The street was busy. Couples walked by with parcels from the elegant shops. Young women strolled along past the shops, occasionally stopping to glance in the windows, cooing to each other at times about something that had caught their eyes. As they headed north, the two men passed by Dickins and Smith department store at 232 Regent Street. Shinwell noted that the store had been robbed by the Forty Elephants two weeks previous. He doubted they would return so soon afterward. The two men continued on. As they approached the Liberty department store, Shinwell took Sacker by the arm. "Stop here, Ormond. Oy see a girl oy know in front of the store. If ya look down toward the entrance, you'll see 'er. She's a little bit of a fing, wif brown 'air, in a blue dress."

"Shinwell, there are lots of young women peering in the windows in front of the store. How do you expect me to pick her out?"

"She's the little one *not* lookin' in the windows. She's lookin' up and down the street. She's the lookout. They must be inside already, gettin' ready to rob the jewelry store. Oy'm goin' to approach 'er. She knows me. Go across the street and come up behind 'er, just in case she decides ta run."

As Sacker strode across the street and circled behind the young woman, Shinwell made his way through the throng of shoppers. As he approached the young woman, she looked up and saw the big man. She looked away for a moment, pretending not to notice him. When Shinwell stopped directly in front of her, she turned. "Porky, you can't be here. I'm on the job."

"Wot ya up to, Silky? Are ya lookin' for peelers whilst your friends are hoistin' fings in the jewelry store, or are ya just keepin' an eye peeled for 'em while they case the place for later?"

"It's none of your concern what I'm doing, so be on your way, or I'll scream you're a masher."

"We both know ya h'aint gonna scream, Silky. So, why don't ya come with me an' we'll have a little chat." As he reached for her arm, she turned to bolt away from him. She ran headlong into Sacker, who caught her by both arms. He introduced himself. "Ormond Sacker, miss, of Scotland Yard. Come with us quietly and no harm will come to you."

"And if I don't?"

"Then my large friend there will render you unconscious and we will carry you away."

"Porky, you know how this goes. If I'm not out front when they come out, I'm as good as dead."

"Nuffing oy can do about it at present, Silky. But oy fink the girls will understand if ya tell 'em ya got pinched by Scotland Yard. Oy'll be your witness if it'll 'elp."

"Of all the people in the world, I can't believe you're working with the peelers, Porky."

"Let's move along, miss," Sacker said, holding a tight grip on her arm. As a carriage approached, he flagged it down. He opened the carriage door and Shinwell climbed in first. Sacker then lifted the young woman in next. He was surprised how slight and slender she was. He climbed in and called to the driver. "Take us to Hyde Park, if you please." Then Sacker turned to the young woman. "We mean you no harm, miss…"

"Silky. 'er name is Silky, Ormond."

"Alright, Silky, if that's your real name, we mean you no harm. We just have a few questions for you and then you can be on your way."

"If you think I'm saying anything to Scotland Yard, you're daft."

"Well, then it is a good thing we are not Scotland Yard, isn't it?"

Silky looked quizzically at Shinwell. "Porky, what have you got me into? I'm no dollymop. You know I'm just a palmer and a tooler."

"Silky, we need ta find out who the Forty H'elephants were workin' wif on the Bank of England job. Oy don't know if you was there or not. Doesn't matter. We don't care wot you ladies done. We know the blokes wot done that job are murd'rers and you got good reason to be afeared, but you 'ave my word nobody is gonna know who we found out from."

"I'm not daft, Porky. I know how easy things could go wrong. If anyone finds out I talked, my life wouldn't be worth a farthing."

Sacker looked at the young woman. "Silky, there is a very good chance the people who were involved with the Bank of England robbery will be either jailed or dead by this time tomorrow. But, to assure that, we need information…information only someone who knows what happened can give us. The people I work with have friends in very high places in the government and, if your safety is your greatest concern, I can promise you I will do everything I can to make sure you are protected…if you help us."

114

"And what if I choose not to help you?"

"We will turn this carriage around and drop you where we found you and you can explain where you've been to Mary Carr."

Silky's expression suddenly changed. She looked at Shinwell, who nodded, then back at Sacker. "I don't know much. There were six of us, picked by a murderous-looking bloke with a Scouse accent. We were told to dress to the nines and do our best to attract as much attention as possible. When they rounded up all the customers and bankers, we were to run out the front entrance before they barricaded the doors. On the day of the robbery, that's what we did. The girls had nothing to do with the robbery. Mary Carr collected a sum from that bloke for the six of us. That's all I know."

Shinwell looked at Silky. "Did you ever hear that fella's name?"

"I only heard Mary call him by his first name. She called him George. He was very well-dressed, but a mean-looking man all the same. If I never see him again, it will be too soon."

Sacker leaned closer to the young woman and quietly asked, "How long ago did this George fellow visit Mary Carr to pick the six of you out for the bank job?"

"I can't say precisely, but it was more than a fortnight ago, of that I am sure."

"Thank you, Silky. Where would you like us to drop you?"

"If you could take me to Tottenham Court Road, I will make my own way from there."

"You gonna be awlroit, Silky?"

"I'll be fine, Porky. I'll just tell them I got spotted by some peelers and led them on a merry chase away from the jewelry store. It's not like I haven't done the same before. Whenever we see peelers closing in, we just hike up our skirts and run like the dickens." She smiled for the first time since they had taken the young girl into custody.

Sacker called up to the driver, "Driver, Tottenham Court Road, please." The carriage turned onto Park Lane, and Silky looked out the carriage window longingly as they passed Hyde Park. Sacker noticed her gazing out at the park. "Silky, may I ask you something else?"

The young woman turned and smiled, "Certainly," she replied.

"Is Silky your real name?"

Shinwell laughed and the young woman smiled. "My name is Sarah Silkirk. At first, when I joined the Forty Elephants, everyone called me Sarah. After a while, Mary Carr started calling me Silky."

"Cuz she can pick your pocket smooth as silk, h'aint that right, Silky?" The young woman smiled demurely. Then Shinwell looked at her sternly. "Now give back Mr. Sacker's pocket watch." Silky opened her palm and there was Ormond's gold pocket watch. "Sorry," she said, handing the watch back. "Couldn't help myself. It was right there for the taking."

"No harm done," Sacker replied, then he paused. "You didn't take anything else, did you?" Silky just smiled. Sacker checked his pockets to make sure he still had all his possessions. Shinwell and Silky just laughed. The carriage turned from Park Lane onto Oxford and then, in a short while, onto Tottenham Court. As it approached Euston Road, Silky looked at Sacker. "Anywhere along here will do just fine. I can find my own way from here." Sacker knocked on the roof of the carriage and the driver reined his horses to a halt. Silky climbed out. She turned and smiled back at Sacker, then stepped close to the window. She held out her hand once more, which once again held Sacker's pocket watch. She smiled and whispered, "You need to be more careful with your things, Mr. Sacker." As she sauntered away, Shinwell roared with laughter. Sacker sat back in his seat, quite astonished he could be taken so easily by a pretty young woman. Then, looking at his pocket watch, he realized there was somewhere they had to be. He called up to the driver, "Seven Stars Pub in Holborn, driver."

*   *   *   *   *

As the hansom cab that carried Holmes and Dodger turned left from Baker Street onto Oxford Street, Dodger posed a question to Holmes.

"Mister 'olmes, 'ow many of them blokes wot robbed the Bank of England ya figger are still in London?"

"That is an excellent question, and one I have been pondering myself. If, as we have been led to believe, the High Rip Gang was involved, it would seem to me they would want to get as many of their men out of London as quickly as possible, to avoid suspicion or capture. Further, if this evening's mission is to simply hand off the stolen money to the organization behind it all, it seems logical that it would only take a few trusted men to accomplish that task. You do not need a gang of men to make a delivery of this nature."

"Oy understand, Mr. 'olmes," Dodger said hesitantly. "But…"

"What is it, Dodger? Something else seems to be stirring in your brain."

"It's just, if the High Rip Gang actually did the deed, why not keep all the money for themselves? Why are they handing it off to someone else?"

"No honor among thieves, eh, Dodger? I presume they were hired to do a job, and likely were paid handsomely in advance by the organization which concocted the whole elaborate plan. I would also presume they were warned of the consequences resulting from any chicanery on their part. While I do not yet know who runs the principal criminal organization, I do know they are vicious and murderous individuals. My understanding of the High Rip Gang is that they are equally brutal, but an unsophisticated bunch of hooligans. I believe they could be easily intimidated by a show of force from a highly organized and sophisticated organization. Moreover, I believe the leader of their gang could see this as an opportunity to move up in the criminal ranks, if all goes according to plan."

"So, oy'll ask ya again, guv'nor, 'ow many blokes do ya figger are still in London?"

"I have deduced it took twelve men inside the bank to accomplish the robbery. The Bank of England is an expansive three-story building. The robbers would not need to bother clearing people from all three floors and out to the back of the bank. They need only hold people in abeyance on the upper two floors, while the vaults on the main floor were pilfered. That would take no more than three armed men per floor; one at each end of the hallway and one rover making sure everyone stayed in their offices. The main floor, however, would take at least six men. Three or four men would be needed to round up everyone on the main floor, bind them, gag them, and usher them out the back door, which is where they were later found by the police. While that task was being undertaken, the other two men would get the vault open, with help, either willing or unwilling, from a bank manager, and begin bagging the money. Once the others were finished dealing with the prisoners, one would go about setting the explosives, the others would start hauling the bags of stolen money to a waiting carriage. When all the money was loaded, and the thieves were on their way out of the bank, the explosives would be detonated, causing the fires on the upper floors. I would think the entire operation took less than twenty minutes. Once the robbery was complete, I presume the majority of the dozen or so men who undertook this job were on their way back to Liverpool before the fires in the bank were put out. The other three or four men who stayed behind went to ground, to a safe house that had been established well in advance. So, I believe we should expect no more than four men remain to complete the exchange."

"Blimey, guv'nor, that must've took a lot of finkin' to figger all that out."

"It is actually quite elementary, Dodger. One only need understand the size and scope of the endeavor to determine how many men it would take to accomplish such a feat. Once you know some of the facts, you can deduce the rest quite accurately."

"It would still 'urt my 'ead to do that much finkin' all at once. If you say we should be facin' four men, oy'll take it as gospel. An' four men ta face is better than twelve men any day."

"Make no mistake, Dodger. However many men we will be facing, they will not be taken without a fight. These are brutal, violent men, who think nothing of killing a man. The bank manager I spoke of before was found last evening floating in the Thames, his throat slashed. I presume since he was of no further use to the gang, and a possible witness to the robbery, they deemed him a liability and ended his life without a second thought. So, choose your words carefully today, my nimble-fingered friend."

"Actually, Mr. 'olmes, oy fink oy will let you do all the talkin'."

"You are wise beyond your years, Dodger."

When the cab came to the junction of Hanbury Street and Commercial Street, Holmes called up to the driver to stop. "This is good enough, driver. We will walk from here." Holmes paid the driver, and he and Jack Dawkins walked along Commercial Street. As they came upon the Golden Heart Public House, Holmes started toward the entrance. Dodger caught him by the arm. "No need to bovver wif this place, guv'nor. Oy knows the landlady, Mrs. Charlotte Cakebread, and she's an 'ard case, she is. She'd never 'ave nuffin' to do wif murd'rers, 'specially if they was outsiders."

Holmes turned back to his companion. "Let's talk to her all the same, shall we? You never know what she might've heard." Then he turned and walked toward the entrance. Before he reached the door, he once again assumed the guise of Cornelius Merriwether, and a noticeable limp slowed his pace. Once inside, the two men moved to a small table along the wall across from the bar. After a while, a barmaid came by and the crusty old sailor caught her attention. "Missy, could ya bring me matey and me two pints of ale?"

The young woman looked at the ragged old seafarer. "Oy can bring ya two pints but can ya pay for 'em?"

The old man reached into his pocket and slammed a fistful of coins on the table. "Will that cover it?"

"Be right back wif your pints, sir."

As she turned to go to the bar, the old man called out, "Is Mrs. Cakebread around?"

The barmaid turned quickly, the color draining from her face. "Honest, mister, oy wasn't tryin' to disparage you or nuffing. Ya don't need ta snitch to Mrs. Cakebread on me. Oy'll fetch your ales straightaway, oy will."

"Calm yourself, girlie. I need ta speak to Missus Cakebread about somefing else. Will ya fetch 'er for us?"

"Yessir, straightway, sir," the nervous barmaid replied, scurrying off through a doorway just off the bar.

After a few moments, a woman of substantial girth toddled toward the table where the two men were seated. As she drew closer, she recognized Jack Dawkins, "Oy should've known. When Nellie came back and told me there was two rascals wantin' ta see me, I should've guessed you'd be one of 'em, Dodger. Wot is it oy can do for ya?"

Dodger shook his head and gestured toward the old sailor, who looked at the woman and spoke in a whisper. "Actually, mum, oy'm the one who wants ta talk to ya. We've been lookin' for some blokes from Liverpool wot done some work at Bank of England recently. We 'eard they might be lookin' for some 'elp drivin' a couple of delivery wagons. We was wonderin' if they might've stopped in 'ere for a drink or somefing."

The large woman placed both hands on the small table and leaned over until she was face-to-face with the old man. "Oy don't know you from Adam, mister, so even if oy did know somefing, oy wouldn't be blabbin' it ta you. Truth be told, the only reason oy'm talkin' ta you at all is cuz you're sittin' 'ere wif Dodger. 'e's been comin' in 'ere since 'is da, God rest 'is soul, brought 'im along when 'e was just a wee lad. And as for you, Jack Dawkins, you should know the person who could tell ya anyfing about them blokes would be Three-finger Willie. 'e 'ears everyfing."

"'as 'e been in 'ere, Charlotte?"

"Oy 'aven't seen 'im today. But this isn't the only pub 'e frequents. Try the Princess Alice, or the Ten Bells, or the Brittania. If 'e isn't 'ere, ya can bet you'll find 'im in one of 'em."

The old sailor rose from the table, tossing a few coins on the table. "Thankee, mum. We're obliged. Tell Nellie we won't be needin' them ales." Then he turned to Dodger. "We need to go."

120

As the two men walked along Commercial Street, Holmes spoke to Dodger about Three-finger Willie. "Unusual name your friend has."

"Didn't always 'ave that moniker, Mr. 'olmes. 'is real name is Willie Abernathy, and 'e was a member of the Dove Row Gang and one of the best thimble-twisters in all of London. 'is only mistake was ta pinch the pocket watch of one of 'is own gang members as a prank. The fellow didn't fink it was funny and cut off two of Willie's fingers wifout givin' it a second notion."

"So, what does Willie do now?'

"Oh, Mr. 'olmes, Willie is still a right proper thief. 'e just changed where 'e conducts 'is business. That's why 'e 'angs out in pubs. 'e waits for blokes to get properly sozzled and then 'e picks their pockets."

"Are the pub owners aware of what Willie is doing?"

"Willie shares 'is take wif 'em, so they don't say a fing. Fact is, some of the bartenders will signal Willie where a likely prospect is sittin'. Course wif all this Ripper business, fings 'ave slowed some, so Willie might be lookin' for some uvver work."

"Whatever happened to the fellow that maimed Willie?"

"Patrick Kennedy? Oh, 'e's in Newgate Prison for stabbing a bloke in the face during a fight on New Year's Eve some years back. 'e and six of 'is gang were in a brouhaha with the Green Gate Gang at the Rendlesham Arms and a lot of folks got 'urt. Kennedy was sent to Newgate and the others got sent to Coldbath Fields. Oy 'aven't 'eard about any of 'em since. And Willie's makin 'is way just fine. If we can find 'im, 'e can probably tell us wot we need to know."

The two men stopped first at the Ten Bells Pub. Seeing no sign of Willie, they moved on to the Brittania Public House. However, their fortunes did not change at that establishment either. No one had seen Willie in a day or more. The two men continued on, down Commercial Street, past White's Row, to the Princess Alice Pub. They stepped inside and, once their eyes adjusted to the dimly lit interior, Dodger nudged Holmes and pointed toward the back of the pub. There, seated alone at a small table, was Willie Abernathy. Dodger led the way to the table and sat down across from Willie. "Willie," he said in a quiet voice, "it's been a long time. Do you remember me?"

"Jack Dawkins. You've grown. Oy remember ya when ya was comin' around wif your da. Oy was sorry ta 'ear about 'is demise. Wot brings ya 'ere?"

Dodger extended his arm to indicate the old seafarer standing at his side. "This fella 'ere is Cornelius Merriwether. 'e's a friend o' mine. We saw Charlotte Cakebread earlier and she said ya might be knowin' somefing about some money bein' moved from the bank job the uvver day. The two of us are lookin' to 'elp drive the delivery wagons if they might be lookin' for local blokes. 'ave you 'eard anyfing about that?"

Willie looked about furtively to make sure no one was within earshot. Then he began to speak quietly. "You're too late, Jack. That job is all tied up in a bow. They got two wagons meetin' tonight in Regent's Park around eleven o'clock. One of the wagons is bein' guarded by some blokes oy never 'eard of. Nasty blokes oy 'eard tell, not the kind you'd want to meet alone at night. The other wagon is bein' driven by some bloke wot came in from Liverpool. Accordin' to the landlord, that bloke took up lodgin' 'ere two days ago and is leavin' tonight. 'e told me to steer clear of 'im. 'e told me oy could lose more than the rest of my fingers if oy tried to lift 'is billfold. So, oy 'ave just been sittin' 'ere quiet-like and listenin' to wotever goes on between 'im and 'is mates. There was a big fella, carried 'imself like a soldier, came in 'ere last night and sat wif that bloke for nearly 'alf an hour. That's when oy 'eard the big fella tell 'im the time and place."

The old sailor asked inquisitively, "Did 'e say where in Regent's Park they were going to meet?"

Willie looked at the old man. "Funny you should ask that. The big fella was very particular about that. 'e repeated it twice to be sure the driver was sure of the place. The wagons are supposed to meet behind Cumberland Terrace."

The old sailor drew two gold crowns from his pocket and placed them on the table. Willie looked at him curiously. "Wot's that for?

"For a few drinks and your silence about our conversation."

"No worries there, mate. Any friend of Jack Dawkins is a friend o' mine. Just 'ope the two of ya don't do anyfing foolish tonight. Ta."

"Ta, Willie," Dodger replied as he rose to exit with Holmes. "It was good ta see ya."

As the two men stepped out of the Princess Alice and back onto Commercial Street, Holmes spotted Wiggins standing on the corner of Dorset Street. The young boy was looking around, obviously searching for his benefactor. Holmes let out a shrill whistle and Wiggins immediately turned and began to run toward the two men. He came to a stop in front of Holmes, panting to catch his breath. "Been lookin' all over for ya, Mister 'olmes. Oy've got your telegram receipts. Billy says they went out first fing this mornin', just like you wanted."

"Good boy, Wiggins," Holmes responded, handing the boy half a guinea. "Catch a cab and head home. I won't be needing anything more from you today."

"Right-o, Mr. 'olmes." As he turned to head back up Commercial Street, he called to Holmes. "Oy'll be at Baker Street first thing in the mornin.'"

It took a while for Holmes and Dodger to flag down a cab along Commercial Street. When a cab finally stopped for them, they climbed in and Holmes called up to the driver, "Seven Stars Pub in Holborn, please, and there's an extra guinea in it for you if you put the whip to it." Then he sat back as the cab jerked forward. Holmes looked over at Dodger. "I know you are not used to my methods, so I will tell you directly, between here and the Seven Stars Pub I will need absolute silence so I might think without distraction. Are we clear?"

"Mum's the word, guv'nor." From that moment until they arrived at the Seven Stars Pub, not another word was uttered by Jack Dawkins.

Holmes sat, staring straight ahead, his eyes fixed on some unknown point in the distance, his mind whirling through the details of a plan he was developing as they travelled the three miles to their destination.

It was nearly one o'clock when the hansom cab came to a halt in front of the Seven Stars Pub. Holmes and Dodger climbed out of the cab. Holmes paid the driver and handed him an extra guinea for the swift trip to their destination. When they entered the pub, Sacker and Shinwell Johnson were already seated near the back of the pub. Sacker waved to Holmes, and Dodger followed Holmes back to the table. The two men sat down and, once their lunch orders were placed with the waiter, the men began to speak of what they had learned during their morning expeditions. Sacker credited Shinwell with identifying one of the Forty Elephant girls in front of the Liberty department store who, after some coaxing, had provided information about the bank robbery and described a coarse fellow from Liverpool, by the name of George, whom she remembered had arranged for the young women who caused the distraction inside the Bank of England the day of the robbery.

"How did she know the man she described was from Liverpool?"

"She said he had a Scouse accent, so I took that to mean he was from Liverpool. Why do you ask?"

"We met a fellow this morning, an old friend of Dodger's father, who told us there was a man staying at the Princess Alice Pub, who appears to be one of the wagon drivers for tonight's exchange, and he too is from Liverpool. While we had been informed the robbery had been perpetrated by the High Rip Gang out of Liverpool, I must admit, I was skeptical. But these two additional bits of evidence seem to confirm their involvement."

"An' like oy told ya before, Mister 'olmes, those blokes 'ave a nasty reputation. They like to draw blood."

"Then we will have to be careful, will we not, Shinwell?"

"Did you learn anything else this morning? While we got some information from the Forty Elephants girl, she did not provide much more than confirmation of what we already suspected."

124

"As a matter of fact, we did. We now know the time and the location of the exchange. However, I would prefer to discuss the particulars when we are all together back at Baker Street this evening. At that juncture, we will be joined by Dr. Watson, Burke and Hobbs, and our colleagues from Scotland Yard. For now, unless anyone objects, I would suggest we enjoy our lunch and relish the calm before the tempest."

There was no quarrel with Holmes' suggestion and the four men enjoyed a quiet repast. When the meal was finished and the bill paid, the four men stepped out of the Seven Stars Pub into the crisp autumn air. Holmes took Shinwell and Dodger aside. "I want to thank you two men for all your assistance to this point, but I will not begrudge your absence tonight, since we will be working with two detectives from Scotland Yard, and I know you both have histories with the London constabulary."

Shinwell looked quizzically at Holmes and then looked to Jack Dawkins. "Do ya 'ear that, Dodger? Mr. 'olmes thinks we're a couple of meaters, afraid of a couple Scotland Yard coppers. Wot do ya fink of that?"

Before Dodger could reply, Holmes interjected. "That is not what I meant at all, Shinwell. You are one of the bravest men I know. I just wanted you to know I would understand if the two of you chose to avoid dealing with the police tonight, especially after what they put you through, Shinwell, not that long ago."

"Mr. 'olmes, let me ask ya, can you use our 'elp tonight?"

"I would be obliged."

"Then Dodger an' me will be at Baker Street at six wif the uvvers, if it's all the same ta you."

"But no pistols for us, if you please, Mr. 'olmes," Dodger added. "Never 'ad any use for 'em."

"Understood. See you at six then."

Holmes returned to Sacker, as Shinwell and Dodger headed off in the opposite direction. "It appears we have added two more to our ranks."

"I never had any doubt they would be with us, Holmes. Shinwell and I had an interesting conversation while we awaited your arrival. He feels he owes you his life a few times over. And I, for one, will be glad to have that formidable individual at our side tonight. I do not envy the poor chap that has the misfortune to meet up with him on a dark night."

"Truth be told, I too am glad he will be with us tonight. We may well be facing a fearsome group of ruffians that will not go down without a fight. We can use all the forces we can muster." Holmes paused for a moment, lost in his own thoughts, then continued, "I presume you will be heading off to your flat now?"

"You presume correctly, my sagacious friend. But fear not. I will be at your digs on Baker Street promptly at six o'clock. I am as eager as you to bring these scoundrels to justice."

"Then I will see you later," Holmes replied, flagging a hansom cab. He hopped into the cab and called up to the driver, "221B Baker Street, if you please.

*   *   *   *   *

CHAPTER SEVEN

Not A Moment To Lose

It was nearly two in the afternoon when Algernon Quartermaine was summoned to the office of Henri Loze. "Oh you've done it now, Algernon," taunted Rene Perrault. "Looks like another one of you English detectives is going to be sent packing."

"Well, at least you'll be in good company. Your friend Sherlock Holmes was the first detective he sent back to England," Remy quipped.

"Not funny in the least, gentlemen. Seriously, what could the Prefect want with me? We have been here working since I arrived back in Paris."

"One way to find out, Algernon," replied Jacques. "Go ask him?"

Quartermaine rose from his chair and left his friends. He walked down the hall to the prefect's office, knocked, waited till the prefect bade him enter, then he crossed to the prefect's desk and sat down in one of the side chairs. "You called for me, sir. Is there something wrong?"

Henri Loze extended his hand, offering the telegram he was holding to Quartermaine. "You tell me, son. This communique came just moments ago. It is marked urgent."

Quartermaine opened the telegram, quickly scanned its contents, and began to smile. "This is good news, sir. This message is from Sherlock Holmes. He has ascertained when and where the stolen Banque de France money is to exchange hands...tonight! Finally, we are a step or two ahead of these criminals. We can lay a trap, retrieve the stolen money, and put the perpetrators behind bars. I need to tell the others."

"Not so fast, young man," Loze replied. "Before we do anything, I need to apprise Chief Inspector Goron of what we have learned."

Quartermaine, thinking quickly, countered, "Sir, do you really want to do that?"

"Why would I not?"

"Two reasons I can think of right off. First, we do not know if the informer within your ranks has been identified yet. If the criminals find out we are on to them, they will quickly change their plans, and we have lost them again."

"And what is the second reason?"

"Do you really want to go to the chief inspector and tell him the person from whom you obtained this information is Sherlock Holmes?"

"You make two excellent points, Algernon. Nonetheless, he is my superior officer, and I need to apprise him of our progress thus far. I will not let on that we have just received new information until we have a solid plan in place." Then Loze rose from his desk, went to the door, and called for the young gendarme at the front desk. "Aubin, go fetch Monsieur Raboin from Chief Inspector Goron's office and ask him to come here at once. I have some news to share with the chief inspector."

After the young gendarme had left, Quartermaine asked, "Henri, who is Monsieur Raboin? I do not recall ever encountering him when last I was here."

"You would not have. He is a relatively new addition to the chief inspector's staff. He was highly recommended to the chief inspector by an old friend. He works now as his aide."

A few minutes later, there was a knock on Henri Loze's office door. "Enter," Loze called across the room. And Monsieur Sévère Raboin entered.

Quartermaine was taken aback for a moment. Though he had just learned this man's name only moments ago, he immediately recognized his face from nights before. He steeled himself as he rose to shake the man's hand. Henri Loze introduced the two men to each other.

"It is a pleasure to make your acquaintance, monsieur," said Raboin.

"Mine as well," Quartermaine replied tersely.

"The young gendarme said you had new information for the chief inspector. By any chance, is this about the robbery at the Banque de France?"

"It is, monsieur," Loze replied. "And it is…"

"And it is new and critical information," Quartermaine interrupted. "And while we would happily provide this information for you to pass along to the chief inspector, I think it would be best if the chief inspector hears it directly from Prefect Loze. You know, the fewer people who know about what we have discovered the better. I am sure you understand."

"I am sure I do not," Raboin replied, indignantly.

"Prefect Loze, don't you think it would be best if you impart what we know directly to Chief Inspector Goron?" Quartermaine said, nodding his head and staring directly at Loze.

Still quite unsure what Quartermaine was trying to accomplish, Loze trustingly replied, "Yes, actually, Monsieur Raboin, I believe it would be better if Chief Inspector Goron heard this information directly from me."

"And what exactly would you like me to tell the chief inspector?"

"Allow me, Prefect," Quartermaine interjected. "If you would please ask the chief inspector to come down here to Prefect Loze's office, at his earliest convenience, of course, we will provide everything we have uncovered, including maps, diagrams, and other pertinent information. And, of course, it goes without saying, you are invited to attend, monsieur."

Raboin glared at Quartermaine. "How soon will this information be ready for viewing?"

Quartermaine turned and winked at Loze, then turned back to Raboin. "In less time than it will take you to go to the chief inspector's office and return here with him."

"We will return in less than half an hour," Raboin snapped.

"Perfect. Let me get the door for you," Quartermaine said, moving quickly to open the office door to usher Raboin out.

Once the door was closed again, Loze stood up, threw his hands in the air. "Mon Dieu, mec, qu'est-ce que c'etait que ca?"

"Henri, sorry. I needed him out of here, so you and I could talk."

"Talk about what?"

"Answer me one question. Have they identified the informer in your ranks yet?"

"Algernon, you know the answer to that question. No…we have not."

"Would you be surprised if I told you I know who the informer is?"

"I would be amazed." Loze stood staring at Quartermaine. "So, are you going to tell me?"

"Monsieur Sévère Raboin."

"Impossible."

"Not impossible, Henri. In fact, I am certain of it."

"How can you be so sure? You just met the man."

"True enough. But, I have seen him before, Henri."

"Where?"

130

"At Le Chat Noir, in the company of another man you helped me and my colleague just days ago abduct from this very building and transport to England…George Harrington Sleeves."

"You must be mistaken. Raboin could not possibly be the man you saw. He…well, he works in the office of the chief inspector. Moreover, he was highly recommended by a well-respected friend."

"Do you know who this well-respected friend is, Henri?"

"Why, yes. I know him well. He and the chief inspector have known each other for years. While their careers have taken different paths, and Felix has been more involved in politics, they have remained close friends. The chief inspector often relies on his counsel."

"Felix? May I ask, Henri, what is Monsieur Felix's surname?"

"Felix Francois Faure. Algernon, while you may not have heard of Monsieur Raboin before, I am sure you have heard of Monsieur Faure."

"Oh, I most certainly have, Henri. He is one of the men who employed Sleeves to orchestrate the assassinations of President Carnot and Prime Minister Floquet."

"Mon Dieu, that cannot be so!"

"Unfortunately, Henri, it is so. My colleague, Ormand Sacker, dealt with Faure and his collaborators directly. He can substantiate everything I am telling you if you do not believe me. But, that is not our biggest problem at the moment."

"How can you say that?"

"Henri, in less than thirty minutes Raboin is going to be returning here with Chief Inspector Goron, and we have promised to explain everything we know about the robbery. We cannot let Raboin leave with that information, or our advantage is lost and, with it, the stolen money."

"What do you suggest?"

Quartermaine thought for a moment. "Henri, do you trust me?"

"Of course, Algernon."

"Good, then give me a few minutes with my colleagues. I have a plan."

"What do I do if the chief inspector arrives before you return?"

"Stall, Henri. I will be back as quickly as I can."

Quartermaine did not waste a moment. He dashed from Prefect Loze's office, down the hall, and burst into the anteroom where his four colleagues were reviewing the notes they had collected individually on the known thieves and ne-er-do-wells of the Paris criminal underground. Remy looked up. "So, do we have to escort you to the train, or have you been given a reprieve?"

"My friends, I have a telegram from Sherlock Holmes. He has provided information on where the stolen money will be changing hands tonight in Paris."

"So, we are finally one jump ahead of these scoundrels," Jacques cheered.

"Yes, mon ami, we are. But, before we address that undertaking, I need your help with a more immediate problem."

"What could be more immediate than capturing those thieves and recovering the money?" Rene asked.

"You are all aware of the fact that there have been suspicions about an informer within the ranks of the Surete, are you not?"

"Yes, yes, of course. But we all thought it was a trumped-up rumor meant to keep us all on our toes," replied Louis.

"Trust me, Louis, it is not a rumor. And I know who the informer is. And I need your help capturing him."

"How could you know who the informer is, Algernon? You have been back in Paris less than a day," asked Remy.

"Because I just came face-to-face with the man in Henri's office."

"So, who is it?" asked Rene.

"A fellow who works in the chief inspector's office. His name is Francois Raboin."

The room fell deathly quiet for a few moments. Then Jacques said quietly, "Algernon, that man is not just some fellow who works in the chief inspector's office. For all intents-and-purposes, he is the chief inspector's aide-de-camp. Are you certain about this?"

"I am, Jacques. First of all, Henri Loze told me Raboin was recommended to Chief Goron by a long-time friend, Felix Francois Faure. According to Ormond Sacker, Faure is one of a number of conspirators who were behind the assassination attempts we just thwarted."

"That is a monumental accusation, Algernon," Louis chided.

"It is not an accusation, Louis. It is a fact. One which I may never be able to prove, considering Faure's position and reputation. But, trust me when I tell you, it is true, nonetheless."

"What other proof do you have, Algernon?" asked Rene.

"My own two eyes. Two nights before the assassination attempts, I was following the Englishman who was orchestrating everything on behalf of the diplomatists, who did not want to dirty their hands with the actual assassinations. His name was George Harrington Sleeves."

"Was?" asked Remy.

"I'll get to that later. I followed Sleeves from his meeting with the diplomatists and, at one point in the night, he met with Raboin at Le Chat Noir. They spoke for a few minutes and parted company. I ask you, gentlemen, what purpose would Raboin have to meet with a villain like

Sleeves? None, I would say, unless he is part of the same criminal enterprise as that man."

The four men looked at each other, each nodding in turn. Then Remy spoke. "What is it you need us to do?"

Raboin will be returning with the chief inspector to Henri's office in a few minutes. Henri is going to tell the chief inspector that we know the time and place of the money exchange tonight. We cannot let Raboin leave this building with that information. If he is allowed to pass along the fact that we know their plans, the criminals will disappear into the wind and the money will be lost forever."

"So, I ask again, what is it you want us to do?" Remy repeated.

"Wait and watch. When Raboin leaves the meeting, I suspect he is going to make some excuse to step away from the chief inspector for a bit. When he does, that is our opportunity to apprehend him."

"What makes you so sure he will want to be excused from the chief inspector's side?" Jacques asked.

"Elementary. When he hears we know when and where the money exchange will take place, he will want to warn his co-conspirators, else they will be captured and the money recovered. It is a simple matter of self-preservation and greed."

"And what do we do with this man Raboin once we have apprehended him?" Remy asked.

"I had a thought about that," Quartermaine replied, with a wry smile. "You are familiar with the old barracks for the Garde Républicaine, are you not?"

"But of course," replied Louis. "That structure is to be demolished soon. A new gendarmerie is to be built in its place."

"Yes, but there are still detention cells there at present, although no longer in use. We could incarcerate Raboin there. No one would think to look for him in that place."

"How do you know about those cells?"

"Your boss told me about them, Jacques. But, that is not relevant right now. If you are all in agreement, I will go back to Henri's office and attend the meeting. In the meantime, if you gentlemen could collect the necessary equipment to restrain and silence our detainee, I would be obliged." Each man silently acknowledging their agreement, Quartermaine rose and headed for the door. "Bonne chance a nous tous, mes amis," he said, as he left.

Quartermaine returned to Henri Loze's office and returned to his chair in front of Henri's desk. "We are all ready for the chief inspector and Monsieur Raboin, Henri."

"So, what do we tell them when they return?" Henri asked anxiously.

"Everything, Henri. We must tell them what we know, or we have no bait for the trap. Raboin must know that we know everything about tonight's exchange, or he will have no reason to reach out to his accomplices."

"But I thought you said it was imperative that Raboin not leave here with that information, Algernon."

"And that is true, Henri. You must just trust me when I tell you he will not leave here with that information. There is one thing I will need you to do, however, sir."

"And what is that?"

"When the meeting is over and the Chief Inspector and Raboin have stepped outside, call the chief inspector back and ask him if you could have a private word with him in your office."

135

"And once he agrees to come back to my office, what do I tell him?"

"Tell him you have information regarding the man who orchestrated the assassination attempts on Carnot and Floquet. And you can tell him he was the same man who tried to assassinate Kaiser Wilhelm in Germany. He was an Englishman by the name of George Harrington Sleeves."

"But, Algernon, that is the man you and your confrere, Monsieur Sacker, smuggled out of the country."

"One in the same, Henri. You can also explain that he was killed…by his own organization."

"*Je suis choqué!* When did this happen, Algernon?" As Quartermaine was about to provide Henri with the details from Holmes' telegram, there was a knock at the door. "Enter," called Loze, and in came Chief Inspector Goron, followed closely by his aide Raboin. "Please come in Chief Inspector, have a seat," Loze said cordially.

"Raboin tells me you have information about the possible recovery of the money stolen from the Banque de France. Is this so, Henri?"

"It is, sir," Loze replied. For the next fifteen minutes, Loze and Quartermaine provided a detailed explanation of what they knew about the robbery and the money exchange planned for later that evening. When Goron asked what steps were being taken to retrieve the money and capture the thieves, Loze turned to Quartermaine. Algernon explained that the plan was, as yet, not fully fleshed out, but the same team that stopped the assassination attempts was, at that very moment, working out the details.

"But you said this is happening tonight, Henri. There is not a moment to lose. What do you need from me to assure we are successful?"

"If I may, sir," Quartermaine interjected. "I assure you we need no additional assistance. We will be ready in time to achieve our objective. The men on this team know their jobs and, like our previous assignment, we will not fail." Though he focused his comments directly to the chief inspector, Quartermaine watched Raboin out of the corner of his eye, trying to detect any reaction.

"I see," said Goron, looking to Loze. "And how many men are on this team, Henri."

"Five, sir, including Monsieur Quartermaine."

Goron, clearly stunned by Loze's response, blurted, "Five! Are you mad, Henri? What can be done with five men?"

Again, Quartermaine responded. "Not to speak out of turn, chief inspector, but these same five men risked their lives to stop the assassinations of President Carnot and Prime Minister Floquet." At that moment, a thought jumped into his brain, and Quartermaine paused for a moment. "Actually, chief inspector, I misspoke. We actually accomplished that feat with six men, the five men currently at work on our plan for this evening, and a colleague of mine who has returned to England. So, in truth, we could probably do with one more man. Would it be too much to ask for you to loan us your aide, Monsieur Raboin, to assist us this one night? I am sure he would be of great value to the team. Wouldn't you agree, Prefect Loze?"

Loze, grasping Quartermaine's ploy, turned to Goron, "Chief Inspector, I think that is a superb notion. Your man could provide additional support for the team, and provide you with a first-hand report of the thieves' capture and recovery of the stolen funds at the conclusion of the effort."

Before Raboin could utter a word, the chief inspector responded. "I agree, Henri, it is a superb notion. Raboin, go with this gentleman, and provide whatever assistance he and his team may require. I will expect a full and complete report from you in the morning."

Raboin, clearly caught unawares, stuttered, "But…but, Chief Inspector, there is much I have yet to complete in the office today."

"It will be there when you return in the morning, Raboin. Go with this gentleman. That is an order." As he rose from his chair, Goron looked to Loze and Quartermaine, "Bonne chance, messieurs."

After Goron left the office, Quartermaine looked to Loze. "Prefect, I believe we have everything we need now. I doubt there is anything more the chief inspector will need to know until Monsieur Raboin submits his report in the morning. I will report back to you before we depart this evening."

Loze nodded knowingly. "Very well, Algernon. Let me know if there is anything else you require from me."

"I will do that, sir." Then Quartermaine turned to Raboin. "If you will follow me, monsieur. I will introduce you to my colleagues."

Raboin followed Quartermaine down the corridor to the anteroom where his four colleagues were gathered around the table closely studying a map of the city streets. The conversation was focused and vigorous, yet remarkably discreet. As the stranger entered, however, the conversation came to an immediate halt. Jacques instinctively turned the map over on the table. "Monsieur Raboin," Quartermaine began, "these are my colleagues, some of whom you may already know. Rene Perrault, Louis Aberjonois, and Remy Bastien, are, when otherwise not engaged, officially assigned to the Surete. Jacques Duquesne works directly for Prefect Henri Loze."

Each man nodded when introduced. Raboin cleared his throat. "I am sorry to say, I do not know these men as well as I should. There is always so much to do for the chief inspector, I do not get around to meet the men, as I should."

"Not to worry, monsieur," said Remy. "We get along very well all the same."

"Yes...er...well, introductions complete, I should tell you that Monsieur Raboin has been assigned by the chief inspector to assist us this evening," said Quartermaine.

"Is that so?" said Jacques. "Let me ask a question, if I may. Monsieur Raboin, are you proficient with any weapons?"

"Why do you ask, monsieur?" replied Raboin uneasily.

"Because we will be facing some brigands tonight, who will not take kindly to our interference, and will probably respond with weapons of their own. So, it would be in our own best interests if everyone here was able to defend himself and his colleagues. So, I ask you again, monsieur, are you proficient with any weapons?"

Raboin, suddenly out of his depth, stammered, "My job for the chief inspector does not call for me to carry a weapon. However, though it has been a while, I do know how to use a pistol."

"Good, because you may have need of that skill tonight, monsieur."

Not wanting things to get out-of-hand, Quartermaine interjected, "Jacques, could you take Monsieur Raboin down to the armory and procure a pistol for him? In the meantime, the rest of you men can catch me up."

Jacques and Raboin left the room and Quartermaine was immediately bombarded with questions from his three remaining colleagues. He held up his hands. "Gentlemen, gentlemen, please, give me a moment to explain. It was my idea to include Raboin in our group. How better to assure he will not be telling anyone about our plans if he is here with us? We take him with us tonight and, at the end of the night, we bring him back in shackles, all neat and tidy. Besides, I have an idea how we can make use of Monsieur Raboin when we get to the exchange point." Then, in hushed tones, Quartermaine quickly explained his plan to his three colleagues. "Of course," he concluded, "we will have to assure Monsieur Raboin does not have a loaded weapon when we arrive. Else, that could prove to be a sticky wicket."

The three Frenchmen just stared blankly. "Qu'est-ce que c'est...sticky wicket?" asked Remy.

"Sorry," replied Quartermaine. "Just means a bad situation."

"Ah. Oui, I understand now. C'est le bordel." Rene and Louis laughed.

The door to the anteroom opened and Jacques and Raboin returned. "Monsieur Raboin is now armed, gentlemen," Jacques announced. "What have we missed?"

"We have just been going over the route for our carriage tonight," Quartermaine replied.

"And what route might that be, if I may ask?" said Raboin, sitting down at the table.

"The route that takes us to Champs de Mars, monsieur. That is where will meet the thieves and retrieve the money stolen from Banque de France," replied Quartermaine, indicating a specific point on the map with his index finger. "The carriages are to meet there…across from the Bassins du Champs de Mars."

"And how did you obtain this information?" asked Raboin, suddenly emboldened.

"That is of no concern at the moment, monsieur. Suffice to say, the information is irreproachable. And our plan depends on it being so. Else, the thieves and the money are in the wind, and we are defeated," answered Quartermaine.

"And when is this all to take place?" asked Raboin.

"At midnight," replied Quartermaine.

"Ah, well then, gentlemen, it seems I will have time to go to my apartment and change my clothes into something more appropriate for a skirmish," Raboin said, rising from his chair. "I will not be long."

Quartermaine replied firmly, "Monsieur Raboin, I am sorry, but no one will be leaving. We have much to go over and, now that you are part of this team, there is much we must catch you up on before we leave. We have but a few short hours to accomplish that. So, please, sit down, and we can begin."

By six in the evening, all the details of the plan had been thoroughly discussed, and specific assignments had been given out. Jacques was to drive the carriage. Quartermaine would ride inside the carriage with Raboin and handle the money transfer. Remy, Louis, and Rene would be positioned out-of-sight and not approach until both carriages had come to a halt. It was their job to engage and disarm any escorts or outriders who may be safeguarding the brigands' carriage. Raboin sat quietly, taking in every detail. When there was finally a lull in the discussion, he asked, "While all of this is going on, what exactly am I supposed to be doing?"

The others looked to Quartermaine, who responded without hesitation. "Monsieur Raboin, if all else fails, you are our *pis aller*. It will be up to you to stop the brigands from getting away."

"Surely you jest, monsieur," Raboin exclaimed. "How am I alone expected to stop a carriage of brigands, if the five of you fail to do so?"

Quartermaine, remaining straight-faced, replied, "Well, let us all hope it does not come to that."

The room was quiet for a moment, then Jacques broke the silence. "I need to go procure the carriage. If you men are hungry, I can stop and pick up something for us on my return."

"That would be good, Jacques. Just some bread and wine and cheese would be sufficient," replied Remy. "Unless, anyone wants something more?"

"I could go with you, monsieur," Raboin offered.

"Monsieur Raboin, I think it best you stay here with us," Quartermaine responded. "I want to make sure you have a clear grasp of your responsibilities tonight."

Raboin bristled at the comment. "I am not an imbecile, monsieur. I most assuredly can grasp what it is I am to do. I am to sit in the carriage and do nothing, unless all of you men are killed. Then I am, against all odds, supposed to try to stop a carriage full of brigands and their armed guards and retrieve the stolen money. A feat, I might add, no one man could accomplish."

"That is why there are six of us, monsieur. And, if we all do our parts, we will all return home safely tonight," Quartermaine replied calmly.

"So, Monsieur Raboin, if you will please join me over here, we can go over the route again. What is it Flaubert said, 'le bon Dieu est dans le detail.'"

As Raboin started for the table, Remy approached. "Monsieur, Raboin, if I could have your pistol."

"For what purpose?" Raboin asked, indignantly.

"I am going to check and clean all our weapons before we go out. Wouldn't want any of them misfiring at the wrong moment," Remy replied, holding out his hand. "I will get it back to you tout suite."

Raboin handed over his pistol and walked over to the table and sat down next to Quartermaine. Louis and Rene joined them at the table, and the discussion resumed about the forthcoming event. It was then that Quartermaine explained he would be leaving ahead of the rest, and the carriage would pick him up shortly before ten o'clock at a prearranged location. Hearing this for the first time, Raboin stopped Quartermaine. "What prearranged location?"

"The carriage will pick me up in front of 228 Rue De Rivoli. We will go from there to the Champs de Mars."

"Why are we picking you up in front of the Hotel Le Meurice?" Raboin queried.

"Oh, you know the place?" Quartermaine rejoined.

"Any self-respecting Parisian knows of the Hotel Le Meurice. It is one of the finest hotels in the world. But you have not answered my question, monsieur. Why are we picking you up there?"

"In the event we are being surveilled, monsieur, I want those watching to think we are the men they are to meet at Bassins du Champs de Mars. More precisely, I want them to think I am the man with whom they are to make the exchange."

"But what if the man they are to make the exchange with is known to them? Will we not then be discovered, monsieur?"

"I believe I can successfully impersonate the man they are expecting, Monsieur Raboin. It will be late at night. They will be viewing me from a distance in the dark. I am approximately the same height and build as the man they expect. I will be departing from the hotel where the man they expect to see has been staying. And I will move quickly from the hotel entrance to the carriage. It will give them little time to assess what is occurring right before them. Since they have no reason to assume otherwise, they will believe what they see. It is not a complicated ruse."

"How do you know so much about this individual you plan to impersonate; his height and build, the hotel where he stays? How do you know these things?"

"Monsieur Raboin, how can you ask such a question? You yourself work for the Surete. You should know how easily such things can be discovered by detectives as accomplished as the men in this room."

"But, monsieur, you have failed to take one thing into account," countered Raboin. "What if the person you are impersonating shows up at Champs de Mars at midnight? What then?"

"Monsieur Raboin, there are many things in life of which I am not certain. But, this one thing I can tell you with absolute certainty. The person I am impersonating will not show up tonight."

"How can you be so certain, monsieur?"

"At this moment, you will just have to take my word for it."

Raboin glared at Quartermaine and sat down again. Louis and Rene pored over the map, discussing the best spots on either side of the carriage pathway to take their positions. Remy returned with the weapons and returned them to each of the men. He turned to Raboin. "Monsieur Raboin, here is your pistol, cleaned and ready for tonight, as promised."

Merci, monsieur," Raboin replied, looking at the Lebel Model 1886 rifle Remy was holding. "Who is the long gun for?"

Remy smiled and replied, "Monsieur, that is my weapon of choice. I prefer it to a pistol any day."

Rene declared, "And we are glad of it. He is a crack shot with that gun. And tonight his skill may come in handy. If things get anxious, he may have to shoot from some distance."

Raboin asked pensively, "You think it will come to that?"

"Monsieur, what would you do to prevent someone from taking a million francs from you?"

"Ah…well…yes, I see your point," Raboin replied abashedly.

"And, monsieur, have no doubt, we do intend to take that money back from them," said Remy, moving to the table to discuss the best sniper position with Rene and Louis.

Jacques finally returned with comestibles and wine. The men all stopped to take momentary comfort in their camaraderie, enjoying the small repast their colleague had procured. Raboin sat quietly at the end of the table. Quartermaine brought him a mug of wine and a plate of cheese, grapes, and warm bread. "Best eat while you can, monsieur. It will likely be a long night."

"Or a very short one, depending on how badly things go," Raboin countered, sarcastically.

Hearing Raboin, Jacques looked over. "Monsieur, I do not know you. Is it this task, or our company that has made you so cynical? Or are you always this way?"

"Jacques, don't needle the man," chided Rene risibly. "Remember who he works for. If you irk him, he might write a bad report about us to the chief inspector. You don't want to be drummed out of the police force after all your years of service."

Jacques, feigning deep regret, turned to Raboin. "Monsieur, I meant no disrespect."

Raboin nodded, "Apology accepted, monsieur."

Then Jacques turned, winked at his colleagues, and said, "But, you are, monsieur, one of the dourest men I have ever encountered in my life."

The room filled with laughter. Even Raboin was forced to smile. Quartermaine looked to his large friend. "Jacques, thank you, mon ami. I think we all needed that to break the tension. Everyone, drink up and finish your meal. We need to be on our way."

As the men packed up their weapons and ammunition, Quartermaine turned to Jacques. "I will be coming out of the Hotel Le Meurice at precisely ten o'clock. Please be sure to be waiting out front with the carriage. If we are being surveilled, I only want them to catch a glimpse of me moving to the carriage. They have to believe I am the man they expect."

Raboin stood up. "You keep referring to this mysterious man they expect to see. Who is he?"

"Is that information important to you? Is it really relevant at the moment, monsieur?" Quartermaine asked pointedly.

"It is to me," Raboin asserted.

"His name is George Harrington Sleeves," Quartermaine replied emphatically and, by the look on Raboin's face, he knew the name had landed as he had hoped. Raboin was shaken. "Is there any other information you need at this very moment, or can we be on our way?"

Raboin replied quietly, "No, monsieur. Let us depart."

"Thank you, monsieur. Much obliged. You will be riding in the carriage with Remy, until you pick me up at the hotel. Remy, take good care of Monsieur Raboin. Louis and Rene, I presume you will find your own way to Champs de Mars?"

"We will be there, Algernon," Rene replied. "You will not see us, but we will be there."

"Good. Then we are all settled on our tasks. I will see you all later," said Quartermaine, who exited ahead of the rest of the men, and disappeared down the hallway. Louis and Rene were the next to leave, followed closely by Jacques, Remy and Raboin.

*   *   *   *   *

At five minutes before ten, a rather imposing ebony Berline carriage, being pulled by a matched pair of Carrossier Normands, drew to a halt in front of Hotel Le Meurice. Algernon Quartermaine strode through the elegant brass-framed entryway and moved briskly to the carriage. He climbed in and the carriage pulled away. After he sat, he looked across at Remy, "So, were we observed?"

Remy replied, "More than that. If I am not mistaken, we are being followed. When we arrived at the hotel, there was another carriage sitting across the boulevard with two sinister-looking fellows standing outside. When you came out of the hotel and climbed into the carriage, they jumped into their coach, and it is behind us now."

Quartermaine banged on the roof. "Jacques, pull over."

Jacques yanked back on the reins and the carriage came to an abrupt halt. He called down, "Why are we stopping?"

"Remy, go talk to Jacques. I cannot risk stepping out and letting them get a good look at me," Quartermaine said. "If our observers pass us by, we will sit here until they disappear from sight, and then we will take another boulevard to Champs de Mars. We still have ample time to get there."

Remy did as Quartermaine requested, and climbed up next to Jacques in the driver's perch. "Let's just wait here a bit, mon frere. Seems we have a follower. Algernon wants to let them pass and then go on to Champs de Mars."

Jacques caught sight of the oncoming carriage out of the corner of his eye. "They are nearly on us, Remy. What do we do?"

"Just let them pass. Once they disappear, we'll move."

The anonymous carriage rolled by at a good pace. It moved along Rue de Castiglione, turning right when it reached Rue Saint-Honore. As soon as it disappeared, Jacques said, "Back in the carriage, Remy. We need to go now." Remy hopped down, clambered into the carriage, and closed the door. Jacques cracked his whip and the carriage pulled forward. As they passed Rue Saint-Honore, he looked down the boulevard to see where the other carriage might be. It was still moving away at a good clip. Once they had past Rue Saint-Honore a hundred meters or so, Jacques pulled up the reins and, once again, the carriage came to a halt. Climbing down, he walked back to the open carriage door window. "What was all that about, do you think?"

"My guess is it was just a check on Mr. Sleeves. It would stand to reason the thieves would want to be sure their exchange partner was on his way. There is a lot of money in play," Quartermaine replied. "Remy did say the carriage was sitting across the boulevard when you arrived. So, they must have had the hotel under surveillance for some time as an insurance measure. Since they did not continue to follow us, I presume they are satisfied Sleeves is on his way. All the same, Remy, I hope you got a good look at the men in that carriage. I have a feeling we might see them again before the night is through."

"But of course, mon ami," Remy replied with a smile. "And if they poke their heads up again tonight at the exchange, I will have a surprise for them."

"Good. Jacques, let's get to Champs de Mars. We need to give Remy time to find his compatriots, and locate a suitable sniper position."

"Oui, monsieur," Jacques replied. Then he climbed back up to his perch, cracked his whip, and the carriage was off once again. No longer concerned with another carriage following their movements, Jacques took the quickest route to Champs de Mars, moving along Rue de Castiglione, turning left on Rue Cambon, turning again on Rue Royale, and then crossing to Cours la Rein, which ran parallel to the Seine. They turned again onto Avenue Rapp, crossed the river, and followed that boulevard all the way to the entrance to Champs de Mars. As they approached, Remy rapped on the roof and called to his compatriot, "Jacques, stop anywhere along here. I will walk from here to find Rene and Louis." When the carriage stopped, Remy picked up his rifle and climbed out. " Messieurs, I will see you later. Bonne chance." Then, he quickly disappeared into the darkness.

All alone now in the carriage with Quartermaine, Raboin sat across from him, and scowled. "What are we to do now, monsieur?"

Quartermaine retrieved his pocket watch from his vest and observed the time. "We go for a ride, monsieur. We have nearly an hour before our rendezvous with the brigands. So, sit back and enjoy the view."

Quartermaine tapped on the roof and called up. "Jacques, can you find somewhere quiet to stow this carriage for a while? We could rest the horses. You could stretch your legs. And we can put our heads together to consider if we have overlooked anything."

Jacques answered, "I know a place." He cracked the whip and the carriage moved along. In a few minutes, the carriage stopped behind a large stand of trees. Jacques climbed down and walked back to the window, crossing his arms, and looking in at his two passengers. "We can sit here for a bit, Algernon. No one will bother us here."

"Where exactly is here, Jacques?" Quartermaine asked.

"When Louis and I were surveilling the park before President Carnot's dedication, we stood not far from here to observe. The tower that gentleman, Eiffel, is building for the Exposition is not far from here. But, this time of night, no one will be around. We are safe here. I will check on the horses. Let me know when you want to head back to Champs de Mars."

"Thank you, Jacques." Quartermaine then turned to Raboin. "Monsieur, do you want to get out and stretch your legs for a bit? You have been in this carriage for quite a while."

"I am perfectly fine where I am, monsieur. I think I will save my energy for what lies ahead."

"As you wish, monsieur," replied Quartermaine, as he climbed out of the carriage. "If you change your mind, we will be just a few steps away."

As Algernon and Jacques quietly discussed the pending event, Raboin finally exited the carriage and approached the two men. "Ah, Monsieur Raboin, you decided to join us. What is on your mind?" Quartermaine asked.

"This exchange you have planned. I recognize what it is we expect to get from these brigands, but what are we going to give them in return? It is an exchange, is it not?"

"Oh, it most certainly is, monsieur. And for our part of the bargain, we will be offering fifty thousand francs to the thieves."

"Fifty thous…where is that money coming from?" Raboin blurted.

"Where it is coming from is no concern of yours, monsieur. Just know it is here with us. It has been with us the whole time."

"Where? I have seen no such money."

"Jacques has been keeping it safe, haven't you, Jacques."

"I have indeed," Jacques answered, smiling broadly.

Quartermaine stepped closer to Raboin. "Be assured, monsieur. We have the exchange money, and if things go according to plan, not only will we get the stolen money back, we will take the fifty thousand francs back with us, as well."

"And if things do not go according to plan?"

"We shall all be dead, and what happens to the money will be of no consequence to any of us."

Jacques slapped Quartermaine on the back. "That's what I like about you, Algernon. You never sugar-coat anything. You just speak the truth, and let the chips fall where they may. And speaking of consequences, is it not time to go?" he asked, as he moved to relight the carriage lamps.

Algernon looked at his pocket watch. "It is that." He turned and headed back to the carriage. "Monsieur Raboin, if you will follow me. We shall face our destinies together. Jacques, take us to the park, s'il vous plait."

As the carriage approached the entrance of the Champs de Mars, Jacques slowed the horses from a trot to a walk, moving unhurriedly toward the center of the park, along one of the two carriage paths which ran on either side of Bassins du Champs de Mars. In the quiet of the night, Jacques could hear the sound of hoof beats coming from the other end of the park. He pounded three times on the side of the carriage. Quartermaine reacted immediately. He drew his revolver and looked over at Raboin, "Monsieur, as a gentleman I know would say, 'the games afoot.' Steady yourself. Things are about to get interesting."

Raboin, seemingly out of his element, asked uncertainly, "What do you want me to do?"

"Nothing for the moment, monsieur. Just be ready to act if we need you."

Jacques brought the carriage to a halt at the north end of the basin, where the two carriage paths intersect. He watched as another carriage approached, followed by two riders on horseback. The other carriage came to a stop, and the riders reined their horses and jumped down, quickly drawing pistols, leveling them at Jacques. One of the riders walked over to the carriage, opened the door, and a tall, bearded young man stepped from the carriage. He stood for a moment, waiting, not saying a word. The two horsemen joined him, bolstering him on either side. Then he strode forward toward the carriage. "I am Auguste Vaillant, here to make an exchange. Where is Monsieur Sleeves?"

Quartermaine opened his carriage door and stepped out. "I am here to make the exchange, monsieur."

Vaillant took one more step forward. "You are not Sleeves," He declared, motioning to his comrades, who levelled their pistols at Quartermaine.

"I am not. But, I am here to make the exchange nonetheless."

"Where is Sleeves? I was to meet with him, and only him."

"He was sanctioned by the organization who orchestrated this endeavor for certain failures on his part. I am here in his place. Now, are we going to do this or not?"

Vaillant did not respond. Quartermaine started to turn back toward the carriage. "Suit yourself. You can answer to the organization and face the same fate as Sleeves. Your choice. I am not going to stand around here waiting for the Surete to arrive. Bonne nuit et bonne chance."

"Wait," Vaillant called out. "Let us make the exchange and be done with this."

"Good. If you will allow my driver to reach into his coach box, he can show you the strongbox with your payment. When we have seen the bank money, he will lower it down."

Vaillant nodded. Jacques pulled the strongbox up, displaying it for all to see. Then, Vaillant gestured to his men. They opened the carriage door and two more men climbed out, dragging three large chests out onto the cobblestone. "See for yourself, monsieur," said Vaillant. Quartermaine strode forward. He looked down at the two chests, which were filled to overflowing with money. "Satisfied?"

"I am," replied Quartermaine, turning to Jacques. "Camarade, please bring the strongbox." As Jacques climbed down from his perch, Quartermaine turned back to Vaillant. "If you will have your men take those chests to my carriage, we can conclude our business and both be on our way."

"I will be happy to oblige, as soon as I see our payment," Vaillant responded.

"But, of course," Quartermaine answered. Jacques set the strongbox down and opened it, revealing the currency inside. "Satisfied, monsieur?"

Vaillant nodded and signaled to his men to carry the large chests over to the carriage, while one of his other companions closed the strongbox and placed it his coach.

While the exchange had been proceeding, Louis and Rene had stealthily approached Vaillant's carriage and were now positioned behind, ready to engage. Remy, meanwhile, had found a sniper position some fifteen meters from the two carriages, with an unobstructed view of all participants.

"Our business is concluded, monsieur, so I will bid you adieu," Vaillant said.

"Not quite, monsieur," replied Quartermaine, cocking his pistol and pointing it at Vaillant. "I am afraid you and your cohorts will have to come with us. You are under arrest for the robbery of the Banque de France."

Vaillant laughed, as his men raised their pistols. "I think I will not allow you and you large friend to arrest us, monsieur. It seems you are at a disadvantage. We have you outnumbered. And soon, you will be…"

At that moment, a shot rang out from the dark and crashed into the wall of the carriage next to Valliant's head. Louis and Rene stepped out from behind the carriage, pistols drawn. Jacques stepped forward, pistol in hand, waving for the driver of Vaillant's coach to climb down. "Are you so sure, Monsieur Vaillant?" asked Quartermaine. "It seems to me, you are the ones at a disadvantage. Now, before things get bloody, monsieur, tell your men to surrender."

"Some of them have already done so, Algernon," said Rene, pulling one of Vaillant's men out from behind the carriage, already bound in handcuffs. Louis then pulled another of the brigands out, also bound up. Vaillant and his other three men dropped their weapons and raised their hands.

Within the span of a quarter hour, the strongbox was back in the coachbox of the Berline carriage, and the three large chests of stolen currency were loaded on board. Vaillant and his cronies were all handcuffed and shackled, seated in Vaillant's coach, the two outrider horses tied to the boot. It was agreed Louis would drive Vaillant's coach back to police headquarters, with Rene and Remy riding inside, guarding the criminals. Jacques would follow behind with the Berline carriage, with Quartermaine and Raboin riding inside, keeping watch on the retrieved stolen bank currency. All things in order, the two carriages pulled away.

"You see, Monsieur Raboin, everything went according to plan. We retrieved the stolen money, captured some of the criminals involved, with only one shot being fired, and no one injured. It was a good night," Quartermaine remarked. "Wouldn't you agree?"

"I would indeed," replied Raboin. "Could I ask one favor, though?"

"Of course, monsieur. What do you need?"

"Could you ask Jacques to stop for a moment? I would just like to step out of the carriage and settle myself. All the excitement has me feeling a bit uneasy. It will just take a moment."

Quartermaine tapped on the roof and called up, "Jacques, pull up for a moment. Our passenger is feeling a bit off."

Jacques pulled on the reins and the carriage came to a gentle stop. Quartermaine climbed out first, followed by Raboin, who watched attentively as the first carriage disappeared into the Parisian night.

Quartermaine observed Raboin and commented, "Don't worry. As soon as you feel better, we will catch them right up. We're all headed to the same place."

Raboin took the pistol from his pocket and pointed it at Quartermaine. "No, monsieur, I am afraid we will not be catching them right up. I do not intend to return to police headquarters. Not tonight, not ever." Then he cocked his pistol. "Tell Jacques to come down from his perch, or I will shoot you right now."

Quartermaine called up, "Jacques, I think you should come down here. We have a bit of a situation. And leave your pistol up there, if you don't mind."

Jacques climbed down and joined Quartermaine. "What is this all about?"

"It appears Monsieur Raboin has designs on taking the money for himself and, I presume, leaving the country with it."

"You presume correctly, monsieur. So, unless you both want to die right here, we are all going to take a little ride tonight."

"And where exactly are we going?" asked Quartermaine.

"I think I would like you to take me to Le Havre. From there, I can catch a ship leaving for somewhere where the Surete cannot reach me."

"I think the Surete will be the least of your worries, monsieur. You are absconding with money that the organization that murdered Sleeves expected to be delivered to them in London in a day or two. And, I can assure you, there is nowhere in the world you can hide where those men will not find you. Even if you make it to Le Havre, your life is already forfeit."

"You let me worry about my life, monsieur. Just get back in the carriage." Then Raboin waved the pistol at Jacques. "And you, climb up to your perch and let's be on our way."

Jacques clenched his fists and stood his ground. "I think not." Then he strode toward Raboin. "I think I have had enough of you, monsieur." As the big man drew closer, Raboin levelled his pistol and pulled the trigger. There was no report. He pulled the trigger again and again, yet the gun never fired. Jacques closed the distance, grabbed Raboin by the lapel of his frock coat, and punched him in the face. Raboin fell to the cobblestone, unconscious. Jacques stooped over, took the gun from Raboin's limp hand, and tossed it to Quartermaine.

"That was either the bravest thing I have ever seen you do, or the most foolish, Jacques."

"It was neither, Algernon. I knew he couldn't shoot me. Remy told me the gun he gave Raboin had no firing pin. Besides, he has always been an arrogant bastard toward Henri Loze and the rest of us. It was time someone gave him a proper comeuppance. If you will help me load this dechet into the carriage, we can deliver everything back to headquarters, and go home."

By half past one in the morning, the Berline carriage pulled up in the alleyway behind police headquarters. Jacques climbed down from his perch, as Quartermaine stepped out of the carriage. As the big man approached, he said, "I think you should do the honors, Jacques. After all, you captured the informer. It should be you who turns him in."

"Don't forget the other charges of attempted murder of a police officer and grand theft," Jacques noted, as he jerked an unsteady Raboin from inside the carriage. "It will be my pleasure to incarcerate this man, and do my part in court to send him to prison for the rest of his worthless life."

Quartermaine walked over to the two men and, looking directly at Raboin, he lowered his voice and whispered, "It is likely you will not live that long, Raboin. Every other man who has been involved with this criminal enterprise and been caught has died horribly before ever seeing the inside of a courtroom. So, you have that to look forward to. Bonne chance."

By two thirty, the recovered money from the bank robbery and the strongbox with the fifty thousand francs had been turned over. A beaten, whimpering Raboin had been processed and incarcerated. The four stalwart police officers were on their way to their homes for a well-deserved day's rest. And Quartermaine, riding a cab back to his hotel, was already formulating the message he would send to Sherlock Holmes as soon as the telegraph office opened in the morning.

*   *   *   *   *

CHAPTER EIGHT

A Visit to Regent's Park

By six o'clock that evening everyone had gathered at Baker Street. Holmes called them all over to the dining table, where there lay a remarkably detailed drawing of Regent's Park, which Holmes had spent the better part of the afternoon sketching on a piece of butcher paper. "While it is not quite to scale, I believe this drawing will suffice for our purposes."

Sacker smiled. "Good thing you didn't have more time, Holmes, otherwise you would have probably built a diorama for us to view."

The other men began to chuckle. Even Watson could not withhold his laughter. However, Holmes did not appreciate the humour. "Gentlemen, we have less than five hours to review this plan and put ourselves in place, so if you could focus your attention, I will explain what I have devised."

"Sorry, Sherlock. Forgive me. I just thought a little levity might take our minds off the gravity of the task that lies ahead this evening, if only for a moment. But you are correct. We haven't much time. We need to focus."

"I appreciate the thought, Ormond. And another time, I might have appreciated the humour. But we are pressed for time at present. So, let me begin again."

For the next hour, Holmes went over every detail of his plan, pausing from time-to-time to ask the assembled company if there were any questions or concerns. Holmes looked to Burke and Hobbs. "Gentlemen, I believe once the money has changed hands, the most likely route for the money wagon is across the Macclesfield Bridge and Gate. It is the closest exit to Cumberland Terrace, and if they are able to cross Regent's Canal and access Avenue Road, they will be lost to us. I cannot stress enough the importance of preventing them from crossing that bridge. So, if you would position the Black Maria in such a fashion as to block that bridge, it should force them to try to escape to the south at York Gate."

"Not quarreling with your logic, Mr. Holmes, but what if they decide to try to force us to move?"

Holmes thought for a moment, weighing his words, keenly aware of Scotland Yard's presence in the room. "Are you intending to be armed this evening, Hobbs?"

"Well, of course, Mr. Holmes. Only a fool would go into this fray unarmed."

"Then, I would say, if you are fired upon, you should return fire…", he said, looking over at Gregson and Lestrade…"in defense of your own lives." Holmes continued, "Now, assuming the criminals turn and bolt for the York Gate exit at the other end of the park, there will need to be another barricade to block their path. Shinwell, will you please accompany Burke and Hobbs to the carriage house? Tell the groomsman, Angus McTavish, that Sherlock Holmes told you to requisition the hay wagon behind the carriage house. Dodger, if you would be so kind as to accompany Shinwell and make sure the wagon has a full load of hay. Then you two gentlemen take the hay wagon to the York Gate entrance and, once it is in place, unharness the draft horse and tie him well away from the wagon. Oh yes, and Shinwell, bring along one of the kerosene lanterns from the carriage house."

"What if them blokes start shootin' at us?"

"Well, Dodger, if you do not want a pistol to shoot back, I would suggest you do your best to avoid being shot."

"Mr. 'olmes, puttin' a pistol in my 'and would be an 'orrible idea. Oy'd likely shoot myself in the foot or end up shootin' Shinwell."

"Oh, don't worry about Shinwell, Dodger. He'll be busy with the hay wagon. You just get yourself to a safe place near the horse and keep your head down."

Gregson stood up and addressed Holmes. "And what exactly will Inspector Lestrade and I be doing during all this?"

"I am glad you asked me that, Inspector Gregson. You, Inspector Lestrade, Dr. Watson and I are going to create an ambuscade."

"A what?"

"A trap, a snare, an ambush, my dear inspector."

"Just the four of us? Are you daft, sir?"

Lestrade caught Gregson by the arm. "Tobias, trust me, this is one of his more reasonable proposals."

"It is not reasonable, not in the least. It is insane!"

"Nonetheless, sir, it is what we will be doing. We will have the darkness and the element of surprise on our side. And I presume you are more proficient with a weapon than young Mr. Dawkins over there."

Gregson, somewhat taken aback, replied with bluster, "I will have you know I am an excellent marksman, sir."

"Then we have nothing to worry about."

Lestrade once again took Gregson by the arm and whispered, "Tobias, please, sit down. You are embarrassing us."

Gregson had one last retort before returning to his chair. "Gentlemen, just so we are all clear, it is the responsibility and sole purview of Scotland Yard to take any criminals that are apprehended tonight into custody."

Burke gave a chuckle. "Inspector, I love your optimism. And if we live through this night, the criminals are all yours." The room burst into laughter. Even Holmes could not help but smile. Watson smiled and nodded at Holmes, relieved that the tension in the room had finally been broken.

Sacker rose and walked over to Holmes. "You haven't mentioned me in any of your plans, Sherlock. What is it you want me to do?"

"Go with Burke and Hobbs to the carriage house. When both wagons are ready to head to Regent's Park, I want you to ride back with Burke on the Black Maria."

"What of Hobbs?"

"I am going to speak to Hobbs. I want him and his Lee-Metford rifle positioned at the York Gate. On the off chance we get an opportunity to put an end to Colonel Sebastian Moran once and for all, I want our best marksman at the ready. I will have him ride back with Shinwell and Dodger." Holmes then turned to the rest of the company. "Does everyone know his role?" All the men responded in the affirmative. "Does anyone have any last-minute questions or concerns?" There was silence. "It is now fifteen minutes before eight o'clock. It is time for us to be on our way. Let us all meet in the field behind Saint Marylebone Church no later than nine o'clock. Godspeed, one and all." Holmes walked to his coat rack, donned his overcoat and hat. He then walked to his desk, opened the lap-drawer, drew out his Webley, and placed it in his coat pocket. He crossed the room and led the entire company down the stairs and out onto Baker Street.

As the last man stepped out of 221B, a small figure came out of the darkness and ran up to Holmes. "Me an' the boys been keepin' an eye peeled, like ya asked. There's no one about, guv'nor. An' the two carriages ya wanted are waitin' for ya 'round the corner on Marylebone Road."

Holmes withdrew a guinea from his pocket and handed it to the boy. "Your work is done for the night, Wiggins. Tell the boys 'well done' for me, and make sure everyone gets home safe."

"Right-o, guv'nor," Wiggins replied, disappearing into the night as quickly as he had appeared.

Holmes turned to the men. "Gentlemen, it appears we have not been observed. There are carriages on the next corner for us, so let us be on our way. I expect to see you at the church in a little more than an hour."

"It appears you have thought of everything, Mr. Holmes. Well done."

"Almost everything, Inspector Gregson. Everything but how to keep us all from being killed. Shall we proceed, sir?" Holmes replied, glancing over to Watson with a look of concern. As the two Scotland Yard men walked toward the awaiting carriage, Holmes hung back a bit with Watson. "Are you up for this, Watson?"

Watson turned to Holmes, a look of determination in his eyes. "If there was another way to stop these murderers, I am sure you would have thought of it. So, if this is what must be done, let us be about it," he said, starting once more toward the carriage. Holmes watched his colleague and dearest friend for a moment as he strode toward Marylebone Street. He thought to himself, "What man could do better in this world with such a friend?" Then he picked up his pace to catch up with Watson.

*   *   *   *   *

As the evening progressed, the temperature had dropped precipitously, and a hazy fog had begun to envelop the night. The carriage with Holmes, Watson and the two Scotland Yard detectives rolled into the open field behind Saint Marylebone Church. "It seems the fates are not with us tonight, gentlemen. It appears we are going to have a bit of a mist to contend with," Holmes commented as he stepped down.

"A bit of a mist? It's more like a bloody pea soup. We won't be able to see anything, Holmes."

"And that is to our advantage, Inspector Gregson."

"I do not see it so, Mr. Holmes."

"Think of it this way, Inspector. If we cannot see them, they cannot see us. Our chances for success have just improved immensely."

"I do not follow your reasoning, Mr. Holmes."

"And that is why you work for Scotland Yard, and I do not. We do not think alike. I would ask only that you trust my judgement and follow my lead, Inspector."

It was shortly before nine when the unmistakable sound of carriage wheels on cobblestone could be heard. The Black Maria came rolling into the field behind the church, followed closely thereafter by a flatbed wagon, heavily laden with hay bales. Hobbs climbed down from the driver's perch and went around to the back, unlatched the door, and held it open for Burke and Sacker to climb out. Hobbs retrieved his rifle from the boot of the carriage, and the three men waited by the wagon. As Holmes approached, Sacker noted wryly, "Looks like we have a little weather to deal with, Holmes."

"Can't put anything past you, Ormond."

Shinwell and Dodger strode up to the rest of the company. "Oy 'ope we loaded enuff hay for the job, Mr. 'olmes. Nearly wore Dodger out loadin' them bales onto the wagon," Shinwell said, patting his diminutive friend on the back.

"Should make for a right proper bonfire, if we need it, Shinwell."

"Indeed. Where do you want the wagon, Mister 'olmes?"

"For now, leave it where it is. Dodger, I will need you to keep a close eye out for the wagons. I expect one of them will be coming in through the York Gate and heading up the perimeter road to Cumberland Terrace. Once it has entered, I want you to fetch Shinwell to bring the hay wagon around.

Block the York Gate, unhitch the draft horse, and take it around behind the church and tie it off. Then all you need do is wait. If either of the wagons returns, Shinwell knows what to do."

"That oy do, Mister 'olmes," Shinwell responded.

"Hobbs, I'm afraid Mr. Sacker will be taking your place on the Black Maria with Mr. Burke. I need you and your Lee-Metford to find a sniper perch somewhere hereabouts. I know your vision will be limited by the fog, but if either of the wagons comes back this way, Shinwell will provide plenty of light for you to see."

"I will do my best, Mr. Holmes. Do I have a specific target, or am I just supposed to stop the carriage by any means?"

"Excellent question, Mr. Hobbs. Yes, you are to stop the carriage by whatever means you see fit. Moreover, I suspect that, if the money wagon comes this way, one of the passengers may be our sharpshooting assassin, Colonel Sebastian Moran. He will not be hard to spot. He is a big man and should provide a rather broad target. If he appears in your sight, please do your best to render him immobile."

"Understood, Mr. Holmes."

Sacker stepped forward. "Hobbs, if you see him, do not allow him to raise his weapon. You and I have both seen what a crack shot he is. Make sure you get off the first round."

Burke nudged his colleague, "And keep that big noggin of yours out of the line of fire."

"Thanks for the advice, gents. I'll try my best not to get shot."

Holmes took his pocket watch from his vest pocket and checked the time. It was half past nine. As the company gathered around him, he said calmly and quietly, "Gentlemen, it is time for us to take our positions. God speed."

Shinwell walked to the back of the church and checked the horse and wagon, while Dodger moved around to the front of the church and found a place of concealment behind one of the support pillars that girded the front entrance. Hobbs shouldered his rifle and started to look about for a high vantage point from which to survey the road…and shoot, if required. Sacker climbed up next to Burke in the driver's perch of the Black Maria. With a quick snap of the reins, the two black steeds responded, and the wagon disappeared into the fog, headed toward the Macclesfield Bridge entrance at the north end of the park. That left only Holmes, Watson and the two

Scotland Yard men. The four of them trudged along the inner perimeter road that encircled the park until they came to Cumberland Terrace. They crossed the damp grassy lawn and moved around to the back of the massive structure. There was still light emanating from some of the windows along the back of the residence. Holmes signaled for the others to wait, while he moved to a place beneath a large red snake-bark maple tree where he could observe the windows without himself being observed. When, at around ten, the last lights went out, Holmes returned to the other three men. "I believe we can take our positions now, gentlemen. Lestrade, if you and Gregson would find a place to hide behind the hedges that skirt the lawn of Hanover Lodge, Watson and I will conceal ourselves over here."

"Good God, man, do you know who lives in Hanover Lodge?" Gregson protested.

"I do indeed, Inspector. Absolutely no one. It was once the residence of Lady Arbuthnot, who no longer resides in that mansion. She is, if I am not mistaken, currently residing on a farm in Alfheim, Norway. So, if you would be so kind as to do as I asked and find someplace to hide behind the hedges, it would be most appreciated. And, Inspector?"

"Yes?" Gregson replied.

"From this point forward, please do more listening than speaking. Our quarry may arrive at any moment. To that last point, when they arrive, await my signal before you spring into action."

"What is the signal, Holmes?" Lestrade inquired.

"It will be obvious, Inspector. Just follow my lead. Now, please take your positions."

With all the men situated in their respective positions, there was nothing to do but wait quietly in the dank, dreary fog. Nearly an hour passed and then, near the York Gate, the sound of hooves and wheels on cobblestone could be heard somewhere off in the distance. As the noise grew ever louder, finally the silhouette of a carriage could be seen approaching in the fog. Dodger and Shinwell stood stock-still and waited for the carriage to enter Regent's Park. As the sound of the carriage faded away, Dodger dashed from his hiding place at the front of the church to help Shinwell bring the hay wagon around to the York Gate. With some maneuvering, they positioned the wagon between the two stone pillars that framed the entrance. Shinwell unhitched the draft horse and handed the lead to Dodger, who led the horse to the rear of the church and tied it to a study maple tree. He returned then to stand at Shinwell's side.

At the other end of the park, Burke had driven the Black Maria some fifty yards past the Macclesfield Bridge and turned the carriage around on the perimeter road near the gate to the Zoological Society entrance. He turned to Sacker as he brought the carriage to a halt. "Do you think we're far enough back that they won't see us in this fog?"

"I think we're fine where we are. But to be sure we don't miss them I'll climb down and find a place I can observe the bridge. We don't want to miss them coming in," he said, climbing down from his seat. He headed off into the fog, moving cautiously along the perimeter road in the direction of the bridge. He was nearly at the bridge entrance when he heard a carriage come thundering through the bridge entrance at breakneck speed. He turned immediately and ran back to where Burke was waiting. "They're here. We need to go now!"

Once Sacker was back atop the driver's perch, Burke snapped the reins and the carriage lurched forward. When they got to the bridge, Burke drove the carriage between the brick pillars on either side of the entrance, situating the carriage so the rear of the Black Maria was facing into the park. The two men jumped down. Burke opened the rear doors, he and Sacker climbed in, and the two men lie prone on the floor of the carriage, weapons at the ready.

The carriage that had entered from the York Gate had arrived at the appointed meeting place shortly before eleven. The driver climbed down and walked over to the door of the carriage. Peering into the carriage, he said to whoever was inside, "Stay put 'til dee show themselves. We don't take nothin' out until dee brass us fe us troubles."

From inside came a question, "Wa' if dee don't show?"

The driver scoffed. "Don't be muggin'. A little fog isn't go'n ter keep 'em from collectin' this rips. 'ellfire er flewd wouldn't stop 'em fe this much rips. Besides, if dee dun show, we'll be minted mun." At that moment, the sound of pounding hooves could be heard coming toward them from the direction of the Macclesfield Gate. A carriage drawn by four Friesian horses drew alongside the other carriage and came to a halt. The windows of the carriage were covered from the inside with a black canvas drape.

When the door finally opened, two men climbed out and stood on either side of the door, each holding a Fagnus-Spirlet revolver. They looked about. Then one of the men went over to the driver of the other carriage. "Hands in the air, if you please." He checked the driver for weapons and found none. "Who's inside?"

"Two guards, watchin' your rips," the driver replied.

"You two inside, step out here, and leave your weapons," came the order.

The two guards inside the carriage opened the door, climbed out with their hands in the air, and stood next to the driver. The driver asked, "So, wa' now? Yous go'n ter shewt us?"

The door to the black carriage swung open and a booming voice came from inside, "Why would we shoot the men who accomplished one of the biggest bank robberies in history?" The man inside stepped out. It was Colonel Sebastian Moran. "We are just being careful. So much money can make men do foolish things. We just wanted to make sure you were going to keep up your end of the bargain."

The driver took a step toward Moran. "Yer rips is all e'yer. We'll be made-up ter tirn it over as quick sticks as we get us brass."

"That is not our arrangement. Where is George Whitehead? I specifically told him to be here to make the exchange."

A voice called out of the fog from behind Moran. "I'm right here, Colonel. And I have my pistol pointed right at your head. Tell your men to drop their weapons or I will have no choice but to relieve them of their boss."

As Colonel Moran and his men dropped their weapons and raised their hands, George Whitehead and two armed men came out of the fog and stood close to their associates. "Do you have any idea what kind of hellfire is about to rain down on you for stealing from my organization?" Moran bellowed.

"First of all, we have no intention of stealing from you, Colonel Moran. I am not a fool. Second, it is not *your* organization. I know for a fact you report to someone else. You told me as much yourself. The reason for this deception is because your reputation precedes you. I, for one, do not intend to be another loose end you clean up after the fact. Me and my men want to live long enough to spend the money we've earned. So, if you would be so kind as to have one of your men retrieve our payment, I will have my men deliver the sacks of loot we have here to your carriage. Then, we can each go our separate ways, none the worse for wear." Whitehead stood holding his pistol pointed directly at Moran. "I am waiting, Colonel. What say you?"

Moran called up to his driver, "Take the gripsack from the boot and toss it down."

The driver did as instructed and tossed the bag to the ground. One of Whitehead's men retrieved it. Whitehead asked Moran, "Do I need to count it, Colonel?"

"It's all there," Moran replied. "Count it if you like. But can we get on with this?"

"Certainly, Colonel. Boys, let's not keep the Colonel waiting. Give him the loot."

Two of Whitehead's men carried ten bags of paper currency and coins to Moran's carriage and placed it in the boot, while the two men at Whitehead's side kept their weapons trained on Moran's men. When the transfer was complete, Whitehead tipped his cap to Colonel Moran. "This has been an interesting collaboration, Colonel. But I hope to never see you again in this life. Now, why don't you and your men climb into your great posh carriage and be on your way. Once you're gone, we'll take our leave."

Moran glared at Whitehead as he climbed into his carriage. "This isn't over," he hissed.

Before Whitehead could respond, a shot rang out in the darkness. "Everyone, drop your weapons. You are surrounded by men from Scotland Yard," Gregson called out, as he ran toward the carriages.

"Ballocks!" Holmes cursed, as he sprang from his hiding place. "Come on, Watson, before that blasted fool gets himself killed."

Moran pounded on the roof of his carriage. "Go! Now!"

The driver snapped his whip and the four-horse team lunged forward down the perimeter road toward the Macclesfield Bridge. Left behind, Moran's two guards scrambled for their pistols and began to fire erratically into the fog. Whitehead's men, thinking they were being fired upon, shot at Moran's guards, striking them where they stood. Whitehead climbed into his carriage and called up to the driver, who had scrambled to his perch during the melee, "Drive us outi e'ye!" The driver snapped the reins, and the carriage took off in the direction of the York Gate. As Holmes and Watson scrambled toward the perimeter road, they could hear Lestrade barking commands at the brigands, telling them to drop their weapons. When Holmes and Watson finally got to the road, Lestrade and Gregson were standing with their pistols pointed at three men, who all stood with their hands in the air. Watson looked over and saw two men lying motionless on the ground. He immediately went to check on their condition. Seeing there was nothing he could do for them, he returned to Holmes' side.

Holmes strode over to Gregson and barked, "What in bloody hell were you thinking, Gregson?"

"You…you said to wait for the exchange and then take them."

"I said to wait for my signal. Did I not say that, Lestrade?"

Lestrade, who had busied himself handcuffing his three prisoners, looked up. "Yes, I suppose you did say that, Holmes."

Holmes, nearly beside himself, barked, "You suppose? You suppose? Well, listen carefully to what I am about to tell you, Inspectors. Get these men off the road…now! Because, in short order, one or both of those carriages are going to be coming back this way in a rush to escape."

As Moran's carriage approached Macclesfield Bridge at breakneck speed, Burke and Sacker steadied themselves, waiting for the carriage to appear out of the fog. Burke murmured to Sacker, "Do you think he's going to stop when he sees us?"

"Well, if he doesn't, we're in for one hell of a crash. Good thing we're already lying down, eh?"

Both men chuckled at the grim humour. But then, their ears pricked up when they heard the pounding of hooves closing down on them. Through the fog, Burke finally caught a glimpse of the carriage bearing down. "It's almost on us!" Both men fired in the direction of the carriage. The rounds whistled past the carriage on either side, but it was enough to cause the driver to pull up on the reins. When he saw the path across the bridge was blocked, he cracked his whip again to spur the team forward, and the carriage careened around the turn of the perimeter road. The carriage traveled as far as the Zoological Society entrance, when Moran called out to the driver to turn around. The driver called back, "Sir, the bridge gate is blocked. There's a wagon with armed men guarding the gate." Moran yelled for the driver to stop, and the carriage came to a halt. Moran climbed out with a pistol in his hand. He walked up and pointed it at his driver. "We need to get this money out of here. Do as you are told, or I will shoot you right here. When we get back to the bridge gate, I will deal with the armed men. Now turn this carriage around." Moran then climbed back inside the carriage and the driver cracked his whip. The horses responded, the carriage was turned about, and pointed back in the direction of the bridge gate.

Once the carriage had passed and disappeared into the fog, Burke and Sacker had jumped down from the back of the Black Maria. They reloaded their pistols and stood, quietly listening for any sound. As Moran's carriage bore down on them, the unmistakable clatter of horse's hooves on the roadway became ever louder. The two men raised their pistols and, when the carriage came visible through the fog, both men fired. One round slammed into the front of the carriage. Another round struck the driver in the shoulder, causing him to grab at the wound. As he did so, he yanked the reins up and to the left, and the horses reacted, pulling the carriage off the perimeter road and into the gravel bed along the side of the road. The four-horse team galloped forward across the dew-drenched grass toward a stand of trees, instinctively veering away when the lead horses caught sight of the trees ahead. The side of the carriage slammed into one of the trees and then toppled over onto its side. The driver was thrown clear of the wreck and fell face-first, unconscious on the ground. By the time Burke and Sacker got to the wrecked carriage, they found the unconscious driver lying a few feet away. When they checked inside the carriage, all they found were the bags of stolen cash from the bank robbery. Whoever had been riding inside was gone into the night.

At the other end of the park, Whitehead's carriage barreled along the perimeter road toward the York Gate. Dodger yelled to Shinwell, "They're comin' 'ard at us." Shinwell immediately smashed the lantern onto the hay wagon, setting fire to the bales of hay. By the time the carriage made the turn on the perimeter road, the wagon was ablaze, and the light from the fire gave Hobbs a clear view of the approaching carriage. He took aim and fired, exploding the oaken backboard behind the driver, spraying shards of wood into the side if the driver's face. The driver immediately pulled up the reins and brought the carriage to a stop. Hobbs jumped down from his sniper perch on the brick wall that framed the York Gate entrance and ran toward the wagon. He pointed his rifle at the carriage and shouted for whoever was inside to step out. Whitehead stuck his hands out of the carriage window to show he had no weapon. Then he climbed down out of the carriage, his hands raised high. "I surrender." The driver climbed down from his seat atop the carriage, splinters of wood still protruding from the side of his face. Shinwell and Dodger strode up. Dodger walked up close to the driver and poked at the bits of wood. The driver winced as he pulled away. "Looks like that 'urts, mate."

The driver looked at Dodger in astonishment, "O' cose it rags, yous bleed'n divvie!"

"Well, Mister 'obbs, what're we ta do wif these miscreants?"

"Take them back to Mister Holmes by Cumberland Terrace, I suppose."

"Wonder 'ow fings went wif them."

"Only one way to find out, Shinwell. Load these men into the wagon and drive the carriage over there."

Dodger opened the carriage door, bowed politely, then looked at Whitehead, "After you, sir." Whitehead climbed in without a word. Then Dodger looked to the driver. "Awlroit, Mr. Porcupine, you're next." The driver spit at Dodger's feet and began to climb in. "Not nice," Dodger said, poking at the splinters in his face once more.

"Can you two handle this rig if I climb in and guard these two?"

"That oy can, Mr. 'obbs," Shinwell replied, climbing up to the driver's seat. He reached out his big right hand. "C'mon, Dodger, oy'll give ya a boost." He pulled Dodger up onto the seat next to him, waited for Hobbs to get settled inside, and then snapped the reins. The horses pulled forward and the carriage moved toward Cumberland Terrace. Dodger looked back at the burning hay wagon, slowly fading behind a glowing fog. "Shinwell, do ya fink we shoulda put the fire out before we left?"

When the carriage approached Cumberland Place, Shinwell slowed the horses to a walk. He called out into the foggy darkness, "Mister 'olmes, it's me, Shinwell. You out there?"

"Right here," Holmes replied, as he strode up to the side of the carriage. "I presume you men were successful?"

The door of the carriage opened, and Hobbs stepped out. "Not sure how you measure success, Mr. Holmes. We have two in custody, the driver of the carriage and a passenger. Not much else in there save one gripsack."

"No bank money?" Lestrade asked.

"That would be in the other carriage," came a voice from behind them. Sacker strode up to the assembled company. "Sorry we couldn't drive it back here, but it rolled over on its side. Burke is standing guard of what appears to be the bank money. There are ten large bags of cash inside the carriage."

"Did you capture anyone?"

"The driver of the carriage was shot and then thrown when the carriage toppled over. When I came to find you men, he was unconscious on the ground. We bound him up, so if he wakes, he won't go anywhere. And there are four sturdy horses we unhitched from the wreck and tied up in a stand of trees."

"No one else?"

"Whoever was riding inside got away before we got to the carriage."

"Damn it all!" Holmes exclaimed. Then, composing himself, he asked, "Who do we have over here, Hobbs?"

Hobbs grabbed the man by the arm and pushed him forward. "We haven't been introduced, he said. "So, maybe you can get him to answer, Mr. Holmes."

"Well, sir, what is your name?"

"George Whitehead, not that it's any of your business."

"Ah, of the Liverpool Whiteheads, I presume. Well, I think these gentlemen will probably want a few words with you. Inspector Lestrade, would you like to do the honors?"

Lestrade stepped up to face Whitehead. "Give me your hands, sir," he said, producing a set of handcuffs from his pocket. He cuffed Whitehead and pointed toward the other three men sitting along the side of the perimeter road. "Take a seat with your colleagues."

Dodger pulled the driver out of the carriage. "Mr. 'olmes, this prickly character was the driver of the carriage. 'ope you 'ave better luck understandin' 'im then oy did. Talks queer, 'e does."

Holmes took one look at the man and called to his colleague "Watson, I think you have another patient to tend to."

Watson walked over and examined the man's face. "Oh my, that looks like it hurts."

"That's wot oy said," Dodger proclaimed. "An' the bleeder spit at me."

While Watson tended to the injured driver, Holmes turned his focus back to the other carriage. "Ormond, could you please return to the other carriage and retrieve the stolen bank money? And, Hobbs, will you please accompany him?"

Sacker, feeling somewhat slighted, responded, "I'm perfectly capable of going back to the carriage on my own, Holmes. Burke and I survived the night thus far, and I am sure he and I can manage to load ten bags of money without much strain."

"No doubt, Ormond. However, I am sending Hobbs with you on the off chance that the passengers in that carriage decide to return to retrieve what they left behind. For if they do, they will come armed."

"Point taken. Come along, Hobbs, we have a bit of a trot ahead of us," Sacker said, as he turned to make his way back to the overturned carriage. The two men disappeared into the fog.

Watson walked over to Holmes, "Do you think I should go with them? They said there was a man by the carriage with a bullet wound. The fellow over there merely has splinters in the side of his face."

"I am sure they will bring him back in short order, Watson. Then you can tend to him. I need you here for the moment, with your pistol at the ready." Holmes then turned and walked over to George Whitehead. "So, it appears the money your mates robbed from the Bank of England has been recovered. So, I presume that gripsack holds the payment for your work. I'm curious, Mister Whitehead, what's the going rate for a proper bank robbery these days?"

"Since it looks like I'm not going to get to spend any of it, I don't mind telling you. My gang's share of the take was ten thousand pounds. Bet you won't make that in a lifetime, Mr. Sherlock Holmes."

"Possibly not, Mr. Whitehead. But, then again, I shan't be spending the rest of my days waiting to be hanged. Murder is a hanging offense in England, you know."

"What if I could tell you who orchestrated this whole plan? Would that keep me from the noose?"

Gregson stepped into the conversation. "That is not for Sherlock Holmes to decide. None of us here could give you that assurance. It will be up to a magistrate to decide your fate, sir, after you have been properly tried and convicted."

"Besides, unless you can tell us who the real architect of this plan was, the name Colonel Sebastian Moran will not save you from the gallows," Holmes added. "And I do not think you have the name of his superior, do you?" Whitehead just stared blankly at Holmes. "I thought not."

At half past midnight, the Black Maria returned with Hobbs in the driver's perch. Burke and Sacker hopped out, and Sacker ran up quickly to Watson. "Doctor, I think you better come quickly. We have the driver from the other carriage in the back of the wagon. He is in pretty bad shape."

Watson glowered at Holmes with a look of consternation. "Is he conscious?"

"No sir. I think he took a pretty bad spill when the carriage toppled over. He was thrown clear, but when we got to him, he was already unconscious."

"He's been shot."

"Yes, sir. Not sure which of us shot him, but one of us hit him."

Watson turned and strode back to the others. "Holmes, that man needs a hospital. He has been shot and likely has a severe concussion. I cannot do anything for him here but stop the bleeding. He needs to be transported immediately."

"I do not wish to seem cold-hearted, Watson, but we have but two working carriages at present. If you take the Black Maria, that leaves us with just the one here. We cannot possibly transport these prisoners and the recovered bank money, as well as ourselves in a single carriage."

"Well, then, all of you stand here and wait for us to return. But I will be damned if I will let one more man die when I can do something about it. Mr. Sacker, will you please unload the bank money from the back of the wagon as quickly as possible. Mr. Hobbs, I will need you to drive this carriage to University College Hospital on Euston Road. The rest of you stand back."

As the Black Maria disappeared into the fog, Lestrade walked over to Holmes and said quietly, "Mr. Holmes, I don't think I have ever seen Dr. Watson lose his temper."

Holmes stood with his hands on his hips, staring blankly in the direction of the departed wagon. Then he finally turned to Lestrade. "I believe that outburst has been a long time coming, Lestrade. I fear I will need to do something to which I am unaccustomed when he returns."

"Really, Mister Holmes, what is that?"

"Ask for forgiveness, Lestrade." Then Holmes returned to his usual confident self. He walked to the back of the carriage, opened the boot, and lifted out a tether weight. As he walked around to attach it to the horses' harness, he asked, "Lestrade, Gregson, will you please handcuff our prisoners to one of the carriage wheels? We are a bit short-handed, and I do not want to have to chase anyone down in this fog." Then he turned to Shinwell. "While we are waiting for Hobbs and Watson to return, Shinwell, will you and Dodger go back to the York Gate and move the hay wagon to the open yard behind the church?"

"Mr. 'olmes, the wagon was on fire when we left it."

Holmes looked in the direction of the York Gate. The glow from the fire had died out. He replied, "Look for yourself, Dodger, it appears the fire has burned itself out. And if it hasn't, you two are clever chaps, I'm sure you'll figure it out."

Shinwell put his arm around Dodger's shoulder and called back to Holmes as they started to walk away, "We'll be back in two shakes, Mr. 'olmes, no worries."

"No, Shinwell, when you and Dodger are finished, wait for us by the church. We'll pick you up on the way back." Holmes then turned to Burke and Sacker. "Gentlemen, didn't you say you tied up some horses back by the wrecked carriage?"

Sacker replied, "Yes, we did. Why do you ask?"

"Since we have some time on our hands, what say you and Mr. Burke go and bring those horses back here. We can't do anything about the carriage, but there is no reason to leave those horses tied up all night."

Burke answered back, "Truth be told, Mr. Holmes, I was thinking the same thing myself. Those animals never did anything to anyone."

"I beg to differ," Sacker responded. "They tried to run us down in the road."

"That was the fault of the driver. And you shot him."

"Oh, I shot him now?"

"Gentlemen, gentlemen, if you want to bicker, do it while you are retrieving the horses, if you don't mind." The two men headed back toward the Macclesfield Gate, which left Holmes with Lestrade and Gregson. "Gentlemen, why don't we move the stolen money into this carriage while we wait."

"Are you expecting trouble, Mr. Holmes?"

"I do not know, Inspector Gregson. But considering the elaborate planning that went into exchanging this money, if I were Colonel Sebastian Moran, I would not want to go back to my boss empty-handed. I would want to at least say I tried to retake it. And if he does return, he will come in force. So, let's move the money into the carriage, make sure our weapons are fully loaded, and stay alert until we get all our people back together."

In short order, the money was moved into the remaining carriage. Shortly thereafter, Sacker and Burke returned, leading four magnificent Friesen stallions. They tied the horses off to the back of the carriage. Sacker walked over to Holmes. "What now, old man?"

"Did you or Burke hear anything when you were retrieving the horses?"

"Such as?"

"Anything...men's voices, the sound of a carriage approaching, anything at all."

"Burke, did you hear anything when we were back by the bridge gate?"

"No. It was pretty quiet. Why do you ask?"

"Sherlock was asking," Sacker answered, turning to Holmes. "There's your answer. Why, do you think they would be fool enough to return?"

"For this much money, wouldn't you?"

"I see your point. What would you have us do?"

"Just make sure your weapons are loaded and keep your ears pricked for sounds of anyone approaching."

The five men split up. Holmes walked toward Hanover Lodge. Burke and Sacker walked back down the perimeter road toward the Macclesfield Gate. Lestrade and Gregson stayed by the carriage, warning their prisoners to remain quiet. The night was eerily quiet, the blanket of fog swallowing most sound. Suddenly, Burke and Sacker came running back toward the carriage. Holmes rushed to them. "What is it?"

"Carriage approaching from the bridge gate."

The five men scattered to either side of the perimeter road, leveled their weapons, and waited for the carriage to appear.

"Don't shoot," someone called out. "It's Hobbs." The Black Maria came to a stop and Hobbs hopped down from the driver's perch.

"Where's Dr. Watson?" Holmes asked.

"He stayed back at the hospital with the wounded driver. He told me to tell you he would find his own way home after he finished up there."

"Thank you, Hobbs. Gentlemen, I think it is time for us to depart. Let's get these prisoners into the Black Maria. Inspector Lestrade, do you want to ride with them to Scotland Yard?"

"I do indeed, sir," Lestrade said, turning to release the prisoners from the wheel of the carriage. "Up you go," he said, escorting them one at a time to the back of the wagon and attaching their handcuffs to the siderail inside.

"Inspector Gregson, I presume you wish to ride with the money."

"You presume correctly, Mr. Holmes," Gregson replied, climbing into the carriage where they had stored the bags of stolen currency.

"Mr. Burke, will you be so kind as to drive this carriage?"

"Glad to oblige, Mr. Holmes."

"Don't forget we need to pick up Shinwell Johnson and Jack Dawkins. They'll be waiting for us at the church," Holmes noted, turning to Sacker. "Ormond, your choice, you can ride with Inspector Gregson and I or go with Mr. Hobbs."

"Think I'll ride with the money, if it's all the same to you. Doubt I'll ever be this close to that much money ever again in my life."

"Hop in then, my friend. And Mr. Hobbs, will you please take Inspector Lestrade and his collection of miscreants to Scotland Yard?"

"Consider it done, Mr. Holmes."

"Then let's be on our way," Holmes said, climbing into the carriage.

*   *   *   *   *

The next morning, Inspector Gregson and Inspector Lestrade returned the stolen money to the Bank of England. There was no fanfare, there was no celebration. There was just an effusive expression of thanks from Alfred de Rothschild for their outstanding detective work. Lestrade was quietly appreciative of the praise, but Gregson insisted on explaining that it was the untiring efforts of Scotland Yard that had brought the matter to such a swift resolution. Mister Rothschild thanked him again and escorted them to his doorway. As the two men were headed down the long hallway to the main staircase, Lestrade asked Gregson to wait a moment, he had forgotten something back in Rothschild's office. Mister Rothschild returned to the door and Lestrade leaned over and whispered something to him. Then he turned and walked back to where Gregson was waiting. "What did you say to him?"

Lestrade just smiled and continued down the stairs. "Nothing important."

At nine o'clock, Sacker showed up at Baker Street. Mrs. Hudson let him in, and he bounded up the stairs. Holmes was seated at his desk and turned when he heard someone approaching. "Ah, it's you. Good morning, Ormond."

"Well, good morning to you," Sacker replied, looking about. "Watson has not returned yet?"

"I have not heard from Watson since he left last night. I believe I have offended his sensibilities beyond repair."

"You do not give him enough credit, Holmes. John Watson may be angry with you, but he is, above all else, your friend. And I do not think him the sort to hold a grudge. Did you ever consider the fact that he may have been at hospital all night with that patient? He may very well be home in bed sound asleep. Give him some time, Holmes. He will be here."

"Perhaps you are right, Ormond. I am just in a mood."

"Well perhaps what I have to tell you will change your sour disposition. I received a telegram this morning from our young friend, Algernon Quartermaine. And you will never guess what he had to say."

"Are you going to tell me?"

"I am. Do you want me to read the telegram verbatim, or just tell you what he said?"

"Just get on with it."

Sacker started pacing about, waving the telegram as he spoke. "Well, Quartermaine said he and his four friends from the Surete had started snatching up every thief they could lay hands on. Then yesterday morning he received your telegram. They set a trap, and caught the thieves making the exchange. All the money was recovered. He said he was going with his friends this afternoon to return the stolen money to the Banque de France. He said it was more than one million francs. He said he will be returning to London by week's end. You did it, Holmes. You orchestrated the recovery of all the money in two different countries in one night."

"I didn't do anything. The organization that orchestrated all that chaos is still out there. And I am no closer to knowing who the mastermind is behind it all."

"But you bankrupted them, Holmes. Moreover, at your brother's direction, the high-placed colleagues of that sinister group, whom you brought to his attention, have been quietly apprehended here in London and will spend years in prison for their part in the conspiracies. Isn't that something?"

"Perhaps, Ormond…perhaps."

At that moment, there was a knock at the door downstairs. The two men could hear a brief conversation. Then Billy came up the stairs. "Mr. Holmes, a man just brought this letter for you."

"What man, Billy?"

"A stranger, Mr. Holmes, an odd-looking older gentleman. He didn't give his name. He just asked me to give this to you."

Holmes took the letter and opened it. He stared at it for a moment. Then he looked up, his face draining of color. "Billy, go see if Mrs. Hudson needs you."

Sacker was taken aback by Holmes' expression. "Sherlock, what is it?"

Holmes didn't respond. He just leapt up and bolted down the stairs. When he reached the landing, he pulled the outside door open and stepped out onto Baker Street. He looked up and down both sides of the street. "Damn!" he exclaimed, turning back into the house. He returned to the apartment and walked to his desk. He dropped into his chair, the piece of paper still in his hand.

"What in God's name was all that?" Ormond asked, thoroughly perplexed.

"Ormond, I…I…need some privacy."

"Of course, Sherlock. Send for me if you need anything," Sacker said, taking his leave.

Holmes set the letter on his desk and stared blankly at it for a few moments. It read as follows:

Dear Mister Holmes:

I have been an admirer of your work for many years. As a rational man, I find your detective methods exhibit a certain measure of cunning and ingenuity. Of late, however, your focus on my affairs has become somewhat bothersome. You have become a fly in the ointment, as they say. And, if I am to be truthful, your most recent interference in my affairs has caused an unexpected setback. Yet, despite your best efforts, you have been unable to ascertain the center of my operations, nor my identity. I suspect that frustrates you to no end. Let me assure you, your actions, while annoying and troublesome, will not deter me from my ultimate goal. I will build the most elaborate and effective criminal empire the world has ever seen. And there is nothing you can do to stop me.

M

P.S. Had you come down to receive this message yourself, we could have met face-to-face.

CHAPTER NINE

Sherlock Holmes Redux

It had been a fortnight since the events in Regent's Park, and Sherlock Holmes had not once ventured from the confines of his apartment in that time. And aside from a solitary conversation two days after that adventurous evening in which Holmes offered a forthright and sincere apology to Watson for his callus attitude, the two men had spoken nary a word. Since then, despite numerous attempts by Watson to engage him in conversation, Holmes barely acknowledged Watson's presence, much less exchanged words with him. Holmes had become morose and, as the days passed, ever more solitary and despondent. Watson had seen this behaviour before and feared his friend would fall back into his old habits, using a seven-percent solution to assuage his mental torment. Watson had gone so far as to search the apartment regularly when Holmes would nod off. Once he had found a small black bag, containing a syringe and a small vial of drugs, in a nook behind the fireplace, which he removed from the apartment. But still he wondered if Holmes might have another hiding place that escaped detection. He spoke with Mrs. Hudson and gave her specific instructions to hold any packages that may arrive for Holmes until he had a chance to examine them. She willingly acceded to his request, herself being concerned for Holmes' well-being.

Late on the morning of November 10, Watson arrived at Baker Street with his usual morning newspaper. He came upstairs with unusual keenness. "Holmes!" he said, as he entered the apartment. "There is a story here about a young woman by the name of Mary Jane Kelly, slain last evening. They suspect it is the work of the Ripper. Have you heard from Inspector Abberline yet?"

Holmes looked up from his chair. "I have not, nor do I expect to hear from him."

"But, Holmes, the man has relied on your analysis of the facts in every instance before. Why would you expect he would not call on you with this latest crime?"

"Why would Scotland Yard rely on me for anything?"

Watson walked over to his friend. "Holmes, I would like to know your mind."

"I would like to know it myself, my friend. I am at a loss."

"Holmes, you need to climb out of this culvert of defeatism you have wallowed in for the past fortnight. It is unbecoming of you. Furthermore, it is downright infuriating to watch one of the most brilliant minds in all of London sit idly by when there is work to be done."

"I cannot."

"Why, Holmes? Tell me why."

"I failed, Watson. The criminal organization I intended to dismantle is still out there. The mastermind I intended to expose and bring to justice is still an enigma. I failed."

Watson slammed his newspaper against the side of Holmes' chair. "This has gone on long enough. You have only failed if you refuse to pursue this matter. If you resign, he wins. Is that what you want?"

"Of course not."

"Then clean yourself up. You smell like an old, rain-soaked goat. And there are two Scotland Yard detectives sitting in Mrs. Hudson's parlor, wanting to come up to see you. So, be quick about it."

Holmes rose from his chair and went into his bedroom. Ten minutes later he returned, clean-shaven, wearing a clean, pressed shirt and different pants and vest. He looked at Watson, who shrugged. "It's an improvement. I will go get the gentlemen from Scotland Yard."

Inspectors Abberline and Moore followed Watson up the stairs to Holmes' apartment. Holmes walked over to greet the men. "I hope you were not waiting long, Inspectors. Please, sit down. What can I do for you?" Holmes said, as graciously as he could muster.

"Well, as I am sure you have heard, there was another murder last night," Abberline began. "A young woman named Mary Kelly was killed in Whitechapel. After viewing the scene, I have to believe we are dealing with the same slasher as before."

"Are there any other details you can provide?"

Moore spoke up, "We got a report this morning from the Commercial Street police station that someone had reported seeing a properly dressed man, wearing a dark suit, black coat, and a black bowler hat near the corner of Clayton Street. It was estimated he was around thirty years old, of short stature, broad shouldered, and had a thick brown moustache. The person said they thought they saw blood on his hands, which he washed off in a puddle. What do you make of it, Mister Holmes?"

Holmes paused for a moment. "Do you recall the day my friend Shinwell Johnson was brought into the Whitechapel police station and accused of killing Elizabeth Stride?"

"I do recall that, yes," Abberline replied.

"Do you recall the description he gave of the man he saw with Miss Stride before she was found murdered?" Holmes asked, now fully engaged.

"Yes, I remember. I believe Inspector Moore took note of it at the time and wrote it down."

"Does it not strike you as more than a little coincidental that the person Shinwell Johnson described to you people weeks ago, and the person your informant described to the police this morning, describe the same man?"

"What are you suggesting, Mister Holmes?"

"I'm not suggesting anything, Inspector. I am saying if Scotland Yard were less concerned with rushing to blame someone, anyone, for these murders, and more concerned with following the facts, perhaps Mary Kelly would be home asleep in her bed instead of lying on a table in the morgue."

"Mr. Holmes, we did not come here to be insulted."

"Inspector Moore, please shut up. Mr. Holmes is correct. But, in my defense, in our defense, Mr. Holmes, we report to higher-ups who have very specific marching orders to arrest someone for these murders. And to do so with all due haste."

"What is the adage, haste makes waste? Unfortunately, what is being wasted here are the lives of poor, defenseless women."

"Can you help us, Mr. Holmes? That is why we have come."

Holmes walked over to his desk and rifled through the clutter of papers strewn about. Finally finding a note he had written some time ago, he brought it over to the dining table and sat down. "After Shinwell was released, I asked him to continue to snoop about in Whitechapel. On more than one occasion, the man you described to me this morning was seen lurking about near the pubs in Whitechapel. And you should know that Shinwell was fairly sure the person he saw was an American, or at least spoke like a Yank. After asking around, Shinwell learned the name of that gentleman. Herman Webster Mudgett was the name he used when he checked into a couple of public houses near Whitechapel. If I were you, that is the person I would be looking for. But I would not wait too long, gentlemen. If you turn up the heat, and this man catches wind of your investigation, I believe he will flee. And if he is a Yank, as I suspect, his flight will take him back to America, and out of your reach."

"We will keep our investigation under wraps, Mr. Holmes."

"I wish you luck with that, Inspector Moore. Scotland Yard is as porous as a sieve. Information leaks to the press nearly every day. It is what keeps the newspapers in print."

"Nonetheless, we will do our best to keep what you have told us as quiet as possible."

"Just do me one favor, Inspector Abberline. If anyone asks where you got the information, please just tell them it was from an anonymous source. I do not need my name bandied about in the halls of Scotland Yard at present."

"We will not mention your name, Mr. Holmes. On that you have my word. Thank you for your time and for the information. Can we come back to you if we need further assistance?"

"Inspector, my door is always open to you. Good hunting."

As the two Scotland Yard men reached the bottom of the stairs and opened the door to exit onto Baker Street, they were met by Ormond Sacker and Algernon Quartermaine. Stepping aside to allow the men to pass, Sacker said, "Excuse us gentlemen, we are here to see Sherlock Holmes. Is he in?"

"You will find him upstairs with Dr. Watson," Abberline replied.

"Thank you, sir. Have a good day, gentlemen."

Sacker and Quartermaine ascended the stairs to Holmes' apartment. "May we come in, Holmes?"

"Why would you need to ask, Ormond?"

Sacker looked at Watson, who just shrugged. "Well, for the last fortnight you have not been pleasant to be around."

"I am fine for the moment, Ormond. Come in, sit down. What is on your mind?"

Sacker and Quartermaine sat down at the dining table and Holmes sat with them. Sacker took a deep breath. "Not quite sure how to start, Sherlock."

Holmes looked over to Watson, "Sounds ominous," he remarked.

Watson put his paper down and leaned over to listen.

Sacker noticed Watson, "Please, Doctor, join us. There is nothing secretive about what we have to say."

As Watson joined them at the dining table, Holmes said, "Well then, let's have it."

"As you know, I have not really applied myself to anything serious since we were in university together. I have lived a comfortable life on the income earned from the estate I inherited when my father passed and some investments which have paid handsome dividends. And the bachelor life has suited me well. But then you partnered me with Algernon here, and sent us off to help you solve a mystery. For the first time in a long time, despite being shot at and threatened with death more than once, I felt alive."

Algernon chimed in, "My background is quite different from Ormond's. I never had great sums of money squirreled away in some bank account, which would allow for an extravagant life. And, the way I was bought up, service and duty were drummed into my brain. So, I have seen war, I have studied police methods, and, until recently, served as an aid in Parliament. But the work I did with you has stirred a different sensation in me. A curiosity that I cannot satisfy by returning to my old employment."

"Don't forget to tell him about the reward money," Sacker added.

"What reward money?" Holmes asked.

"Banque de France was very appreciative of our work in returning all their stolen money. My colleagues and I were each given a reward for our involvement. My share amounted to three thousand pounds."

"Congratulations, my boy," Watson exclaimed. "Well-deserved."

"I don't understand. What does all this have to do with you coming here?"

"Ah, yes. Well, Sherlock, Quartermaine and I have been discussing a possible partnership, but we wanted to get your blessing first."

"Why in the world would you need my blessing for anything?"

"Quartermaine and I want to open a detective agency, Sherlock. But, if you object for any reason, we will reconsider."

Holmes leaned back in his chair. He thought for a moment. Then, "I have a few questions, gentlemen."

"Of course. We will do our best to answer."

"What type of detective agency are you planning? Are you going to be a competitor of mine? Or are you planning to be more like Pinkerton's?"

Quartermaine responded, "We are definitely not going to be like the Pinkerton Agency. I don't believe we have the resources to compete with them. Nor is it our intention to solicit large companies for day-to-day protection."

"So, you intend to compete with me?"

"Don't be ridiculous, Holmes," Sacker replied. "We do not have your reputation, your years of experience, your connections, and, most of all, we do not have you. We simply want to start a detective agency that can help people who have simple requests, a missing person, a stolen brooch, a wayward spouse. Nothing on the order of what you undertake. We just want to keep our hands in. What say you?"

A smile slowly crept across Holmes' face. "I say, Bravo! I could not think of two more worthy colleagues. What do you think, Watson?"

Watson seconded Holmes' approval. "I believe you two gentlemen will make fine detectives in your own right. Have you found a place to set up shop yet?"

"Not yet," Sacker replied. "We needed first to get over this hurdle. But it will be our next order of business when we are concluded here."

"Well, I wish you great success, my friends, But I would ask one favor."

"Anything, Sherlock," Sacker replied, genuinely.

"In the event I run into some trouble and need some able-bodied detectives to assist, can I call on you two to help an old consulting detective solve a case or two?"

Quartermaine looked at Sacker. They both smiled. "Absolutely," they said in unison.

"Thank you, Sherlock," Sacker said, rising from the dining table. "You have always been a great friend."

"As have you, Ormond. Let me know when you are settled in your new digs. I want to come by and see how a proper detective agency should look."

The two men left, and Watson returned to his favorite chair. He picked up his newspaper and continued where he had left off. Holmes walked to his desk and sat, staring out the window at the flat grey sky. "What am I going to do, Watson? My mind rebels at stagnation."

"Holmes, your friends have not yet been gone five minutes and you are already drifting back to that place in your brain that drains you of all ambition. What did you once say to me, 'Give me problems, give me work, give me the most intricate analysis, and I am in my proper atmosphere.' What more intricate a problem could you devise than trying to learn the identity of the person who left you that blasted note. Stop lamenting and get to work. I am no detective, but even I can see you have clues which should give you something to go on."

"What are you talking about? What clues?"

Holmes, what is it you have said to me, you see but you do not observe. I will go you one better, you hear but you do not listen."

"That is ridiculous, Watson."

"Is it? You have a letter on your desk which has been driving you to distraction for more than a fortnight. You have pored over every sentence,

189

every word, when the most important clue, to my mind, is one solitary letter – an M. And, when Sacker returned from his excursion with that man, Sleeves, he reported back to you that Sleeves had witnessed Colonel Moran shoot a man for disloyalty and his last words to the man were 'compliments of the professor.' I have seen you solve crimes with far weaker clues."

The room was quiet for a good long time after that exchange. Finally, at around five o'clock, Watson set his newspaper aside and rose from his chair. "Holmes, I cannot stand the pong of pipe smoke a moment longer. Make yourself presentable. We are going out."

"And where might we be going?"

"Anywhere but inside this bloody room." As he spoke, a thought struck him. "You are coming with me. We are going to take a carriage to fetch Mary, and the three of us are going to dinner. And I will have no truck with your excuses. Get yourself ready while I flag a carriage for us." Watson glared at Holmes until he rose from his desk, then strode across the apartment, descended the stairs, and stepped onto Baker Street to hail a carriage. Within an hour, Holmes, Watson, and Mary Morstan were properly seated in a red velvet-lined booth in Rules. The food was fit for royalty, the conversation was cheerful, and even the melancholy Sherlock Holmes could not help but delight in the company of his dear friends, albeit for one fleeting evening. At night's end, Holmes climbed the stairs to his apartment, walked to his bedroom and, for the first time in longer than he could remember, found himself climbing into bed, instead of staring into the dark London night.

The next day, the weather had taken a sudden turn to rain, with high autumnal winds. Watson arrived shortly before noon. His shoulder, which had been shattered by a Jezail bullet during his time in Afghanistan, was throbbing with dull persistence. As he entered the apartment, he found Holmes seated at his desk writing in his notebook. "Working on your monograph regarding the use of disguises in crime detection again, Holmes? Or has something else caught your fancy?"

"Actually, Watson, I was working on a new monograph, the utility of dogs in detective work."

"And I suppose you are going to immortalize that ugly, long-haired, lop-eared mongrel Toby as a sterling example of such an animal."

"And why not? Despite what you may think of that hound, Watson, he has served me well often and is, as you put it, a sterling example. There have been times when I would rather have Toby's help than that of the whole detective force in London."

"I will not argue the point with you, Holmes. I am happy just to see you engaging your brain."

The afternoon passed without a single disturbance. Watson read his paper and then fell asleep in his armchair. Holmes wrote quietly, pausing briefly from time-to-time to recall salient events from his past, or to refill his briarwood pipe. Shortly before 3 p.m., Holmes opened his desk drawer and withdrew a letter he had received only the day before. He pored over the contents again, then crossed to a sleeping Watson. He tapped him gently on the shoulder. Watson stirred from his nap. "What is it, Holmes."

"I have a letter here in my hand from Lord St. Simon. I will read it to you." Then Holmes proceeded to divulge the contents. Once concluded, he began to fold up the missive, and he added offhandedly, "It is from Grosvenor Mansions, written with a quill pen, and the noble lord has had the misfortune to get a smear of ink upon the outside of his right little finger."

"Holmes, he said he would be here today at four o'clock. It is three now. He will be here in an hour."

"Then I just have time, with your assistance, to get clear upon the subject." Then Holmes went to his desk and retrieved a packet of documents. He carried them to the dining table and the two men pored over the papers, discussing one item, then the next, and so forth. Then, a few minutes after four, there was a ring at the bell. "I have no doubt this will prove to be our noble client. Do not dream of going, Watson, for I very much prefer having a witness, if only as a check to my own memory."

Mrs. Hudson could be heard talking with someone and then the sound of Billy bounding up the stairs followed. When he broached the doorway, he said, "Mr. Holmes, there is a man here to see you. He says his name is Lord Robert St. Simon, Mr. Holmes. He appears to be a right proper gentleman. Shall I send him up?"

"Please show him up, Billy," Holmes replied, standing and walking over to his coatrack to don his suitcoat.

A few moments passed and Billy threw open the door again. "Lord Robert St. Simon," he announced, stepping aside. Lord Robert St. Simon came up the stairs and stopped at the threshold of the doorway. He was, by all appearances, a well-dressed English gentleman. He had a pleasant, cultured face, with a long, straight nose, and clear eyes, but a man of obvious advanced age, with a slight stoop in his stance and a bend in his knees when he walked. His bearing was brisk, that of a man who had been accustomed, all of his life, to giving orders and being obeyed. "May I come in, Mister Holmes?" he asked. He advanced slowly into the room, turning his head from left to right, and swinging in his right hand the cord which held his golden eye glasses.

"Good day, Lord St. Simon," Holmes said, bowing politely. "Please, sir, come in. Pray, take the basket chair. This is my friend and colleague, Dr. John Watson. Draw up a little to the fire and we will talk your matter over," Holmes implored. "Would you like a spot of tea?"

"No thank you, sir. I have come to speak to you about a most painful matter to me. I have been cut to the quick. I need you to find my bride," Lord Robert said, quietly, clearly embarrassed. "I understand you have already resolved several delicate cases of this sort, though I hardly presume they were from the same class of society."

Holmes, clearly insulted by the inference, responded, "No, I am descending."

"I beg pardon."

"My last client of the sort was a king."

"Oh really! I had no idea. And which king, may I ask?'

"The King of Scandinavia."

"What! Had he lost his wife?" Lord St. Simon asked, astonished.

"You can understand," said Holmes suavely, "I extend to the affairs of my other clients the same secrecy which I promise to you in yours." Holmes looked over at Watson, who was scribing every word in his notebook. They nodded to each other. "Let us continue. When did your bride vanish?"

"On the morning of our wedding. Mr. Holmes, I must tell you that Inspector G. Lestrade of Scotland Yard has already been engaged in this case, but I am desperate to resolve this matter as soon as possible. That is why I have come to you."

"I understand, Lord St. Simon. Inspector Lestrade is a good man, but I am sure we can provide the assistance you require in this matter."

After a lengthy conversation, in which Holmes drew out every detail he thought relevant, he looked to Lord St. Simon, "I do not think I need detain you any longer. I shall communicate with you."

As the gentleman disappeared down the seventeen stairs to the landing that opened out to Baker Street, Holmes crossed the room. He walked to his desk, opened the lap drawer, and withdrew his pen knife from his desk. He walked to the dining table and retrieved the contemptuous letter from M from beneath one of two books which lay open there. As he pulled on the letter, the book flopped closed. For the first time, Watson could see the title – *A Treatise Upon the Binomial Theorem*. He walked over and picked up the other book, the title of which was *The Dynamics of an Asteroid*. He looked at the author's name, and was about to say something, when Holmes, with one thrust, plunged the pen knife through the letter and stuck it to the wall above his desk.

Watson looked at Holmes. "Angst?"

Holmes shook his head. "Incentive."

*   *   *   *   *

*** To Be Concluded ***